Family Harmony
Book 2: The Montgomery Family Chronicles

J.J. Massa

Published by
Melange Books, LLC
White Bear Lake, MN 55110
www.melange-books.com

ISBN **978-1-61235-147-6**
The Montgomery Family Chronicles, Book 2: Family Harmony,
J.J. Massa Copyright © 2007-2009, 2011

Credits

Editor: Nancy Schumacher
Copy Editor: Mae Powers
Format Editor: Mae Powers
Cover Artist: A. Bratt

Family Harmony
Book 2: The Montgomery
Family Chronicles

J.J. Massa

Dedication:

To all of my readers. Thank you for your never-ending support.

Lakon Montgomery tried to avoid Mya Brooks, the beautiful Englishwoman who had the voice of an angel, but he can't resist her. She was destined to be his mate and he is powerless to stop himself. Just when he's getting closer to Mya, his brother and his own primal instincts scare her away. What will Lakon have to do to get her back? Will her family, and his, keep them apart forever? With Mya out of reach, how will Lakon protect Mya from the evil that stalks her?

www.jjmassa.com

Melange Digest, Short Story: Nailed

Vampire Anthology: Slow Burn
Vampire Novel: Counting Midnight
Vampire Anthology: Dark Blood

The Montgomery Family Chronicles:
Book 1, Acting Like Family (Werewolf Series)

Family Harmony
Book 2: The Montgomery
Family Chronicles
By J.J. Massa

Prologue

The moon hung low in the purple grey sky and the trilling sound of morning birds seemed almost at odds with the picture it made. Mya could hear the distant rustle of bushes and thought she saw a large animal disappear into the shadows.

"What're you looking at, pet?"

Mya jerked and clutched her hand to her heart. "You scared the wee out of me, Myles. I thought you were asleep!"

"Nice image," her brother snarked half-heartedly, shifting to fold his arms behind his head. "We'll be in Virginia by lunchtime. How're you holding up?"

"I'm okay, My," she assured him, rolling onto her back so that the top of her head touched the crown of his. "I just couldn't stand being cooped up in there anymore. I mean, as long as the bus was parked, why should we stay in it?"

"I'm not arguing with you, love. I'm right here with you, after all. You feeling guilty because his highness passed an edict and we ignored it as usual? 'S not like it's the first time."

He was right of course; just because Lakon Montgomery told them they had to do something or other did not mean she was in agreement with that. After all, what he didn't know wouldn't hurt him, right? But she he wasn't about to be obvious about it. The man was quite forceful, and somewhat threatening, though Mya thought he was attractive, too.

"Hey, we didn't leave the bus, now did we? We're still on the bus…"

"I think he said to stay *in* the bus, pet," Myles snickered and rolled to his side, propping himself up with one elbow. "But the view really is much better from here on top of it."

She grinned cheekily over at him, turning over to her side so that she faced the same way he did. "It certainly is. And it's a good thing he doesn't know about this, or we'd have to pay extra for it, a pound of flesh at least—instead of him paying us to be here."

Mya chuckled quietly when Myles reached back and tweaked her nose. With a half-hearted sigh, she pushed herself to her knees and crawled carefully to the edge of the bus. It wasn't unusual during the frequent state-to-state tours for the drivers to pull the busses off to the side on some deserted highway and declare themselves to be 'on break'.

The boss, Lakon Montgomery, had told them all that those employees who weren't bus drivers, or otherwise notified, should stay on board the busses for the few hours they sat still.

Generally, the busses were left idling, or whatever they did to allow power to stay on. Mya really didn't know all about those things, nor did she care. She could read, go to the bathroom, have air conditioning when it was hot, and those things were nice. But she'd never really liked being contained. So when she was told to stay put, she automatically felt the need to get out. Myles was just the same way, which was no surprise since they were twins.

Because of all the things they had in common, one look was all it took to ensure they were in perfect agreement. As soon as the two were alone, they decided to watch, wait, and see what happened when the bus drivers got out, and then they'd find a way around the constricting new rule. It wasn't as if this happened every other day. That wasn't the point.

The first time they'd had what soon became referred to as layovers, each watched from opposite sides of the bus, Myles with the male crew members, Mya with the females. There were three each assigned to their bus, aside from Myles and Mya. It was a pretty large group.

The drivers had milled around, four altogether, and a handful of other people, too, including Lakon Montgomery, the boss. The group of them had walked together around a stand of trees, talking to each other quietly.

After watching for several stops, Mya and Myles determined that the layovers were never longer than four hours, but always as long as three. Also, the stops were always scheduled for late at night, nearly midnight each time.

Nowadays when the busses stopped for a layover, brother and sister now habitually waited twenty or thirty minutes, slipped out their respective windows, and climbed to the roof of the bus to enjoy the night air. A close eye was kept on the time and the twins made sure they were back in their assigned bunks with a half hour or more to spare. So far, they'd never been caught, nor had they seen where the drivers or their companions had disappeared to during these breaks.

The layovers seldom took place on days when it was raining. On the few occasions that there happened to be snow, however, the twins found that it was apparently not a deterrent for the layover. Myles and Mya stayed inside on those nights. It would have been too obvious then to sneak out. There was no fun in thumbing your nose at authority if you were setting yourself up to get caught. And neither of them really wanted to get caught, they simply wanted the freedom of choice. It didn't have to make sense to anyone besides themselves.

Chapter 1

The amphitheater was all but empty, only a few of the eleven thousand seats occupied by staff, reporters, or various unidentified technicians. Lakon Montgomery was in the middle of rehearsing his current number-one hit when a movement off to his left caught his eye. Specifically, a perfectly shaped, denim covered, feminine derriere drew his attention away from the business at hand.

Stumbling through the well known stanza, he half-heartedly plucked at his guitar as the young lady emerged from behind an enormous speaker. The lead singer from the opening band walked over, noticing the direction of his gaze, a pitying smirk tilting his lips.

"Don't even bother, hoss. She won't give you the time of day," the man laughed at him shaking his head.

As Lakon moved his eyes back to the girl, he saw another man join her, extending a hand and helping her to her feet. The newcomer and the girl bore a strong resemblance to each other, leaving Lakon to vaguely hope they were related somehow. She wasn't a Were, he knew that. Why did he care about this other guy touching her?

"C'mon, luvvie, let's go to the beach and see just how many clothes each of us has to shed to cause an incident," the young man suggested playfully.

"Loser buys the booze, right?" the girl laughed. "I have every intention of getting pissed tonight." Lakon furrowed his brow. She didn't look mad...

"Guess you'd better get your tiniest bib, eh?" he elbowed her, and then reached for her hand. "It's the only way you'll be getting *me* to pay. Not that I expect you to win this one."

"Guess you better get your biggest pair of socks, eh?" She elbowed him back, her fingers dropping to twine with his. "Maybe the ladies or the nancy boys will notice you," she giggled.

When the couple walked away, Lakon reluctantly turned back to the other singer.

"Who was that?" he asked. He'd never really noticed her before. In fact, it was almost as if the two were *trying* not to be noticed.

"You don't know?" the man asked incredulously. "They work for *you*, man! She does sound, her brother does lights, or vice versa. Whatever. I'll catch ya later—I'm following them to the beach. I may never get to touch that sweet thing, but at least I can look." The other man left. Lakon couldn't help but notice that two other members of the man's band followed him, guilty looks on their faces.

Fighting his body's reaction to the image of that delectable body in a skimpy bikini, Lakon stood staring after the girl and inhaling the intriguing scent she'd left behind.

He wasn't crazy about the idea of the other singer and his friends following the young woman either. Of course, her brother would keep an eye on her. And even if he didn't, what business was it of Lakon's? None. It was not his business at all.

Nonetheless, he found himself staring after her until the two siblings slipped completely out of sight. The backup band's singer who'd taken off after them was nowhere to be seen, either. From the looks exchanged, he didn't know who the man's crewmembers were following, brother or sister…

It didn't matter. They were part of Lakon's crew and it was not a good idea for him to be chasing after the hired help. It just started rumors—rumors that Lakon could certainly do without. If he wanted a roll in the hay, there were plenty of women; Weres from his pack as a matter of fact, who were all too happy to meet his needs. And not a one of them would tell tales out of school.

With that in mind, Lakon turned away from the direction the others had gone and fished his cell out of his pocket. That young woman would fade from his mind as soon as he took care of his body's pressing needs. Her scent tickled and teased at him still, but it was nothing important—he could ignore it. No doubt, she used a new brand of perfume, or possibly an old one he'd never heard of before, just as he'd never noticed her before. He'd gone this long without worrying about the woman or becoming aware of her sweet scent—he damn sure wouldn't let it bother him now.

As he made his way back toward his trailer, Lakon pulled out his cell phone, wondering what Riker and the boys were doing right then. It was past time for a visit to Montgomery Mountain. He hadn't seen his family in months. Maybe he should give Tav a call instead of finding a warm female body for the night. It would be less complicated and he really didn't feel like sex with a stranger right now.

"Yancey!" he shouted, stuffing his cell back into his pocket. In his current mood, a phone call to anyone was a bad idea. At least Yancey got paid to put up with him.

"What is it, Lake?" He spun around. Yancey had apparently been nearby, watching him. A half smile played about the man's mouth and Lakon had a brief desire to knock it off of him. Yancey Livingston, his manager, cousin and fellow werewolf, arched a dark red brow at him. "Bad mood? I thought you were enjoying the scenery there for a minute…what happened?"

Lakon released an inarticulate snarl, not even sure what to say. Thankfully, he didn't need to say a thing.

"We'll go for a run later. We can be back in plenty of time for the show. How's that sound?"

Lakon sighed in relief. "Yeah. Sounds good."

* * * *

It was two-thirty in the morning, and Lakon was surprised to hear voices as he and Yancey slipped into the concert hall. They'd been out hunting on this, their first night in Philadelphia, and had just transformed back to human form. Both had left clothes in Lakon's dressing room and the two thought they could come and go unnoticed. Usually after two in the morning, the area was deserted.

"Who's here?" Lakon asked Yancey once they'd reached his dressing room. They hadn't been spotted.

"It's got to be Mya and Myles Brooks. They do lights, sound, and set design. They write a little, too," Yancey explained. He pronounced her name Mie-ah. "They like to work when nobody's around. They're good at what they do. Not to mention the fact that they look good doing it—at least you seemed to think so earlier today," Yancey said, aiming a knowing smirk in Lakon's direction. " Wanna let them know we're here?"

"Naw," answered Lakon. "I've always wanted to see how they figure out what colors to use."

The two men quietly eased into the amphitheater's seating area, but stayed back in the darkness.

For a few minutes, they watched and listened as Myles manipulated lights from a booth near the ceiling while Mya danced around the stage calling out colors. They could hear Lakon's own voice singing as it was played over the sound system.

Watching from the shadows, Lakon couldn't take his eyes off the small brunette beauty whose lissome body floated across the stage. Her long, artfully mussed, sable colored hair shifted in the pale light and begged for a man to plunge his hands into it.

She had an oval face enhanced by a dainty chin, elegant cheekbones, and well-shaped, delicate eyebrows. Her eyes were a rich light brown the color of aged bourbon, rimmed by impossibly long lashes. Lakon's eyes devoured every detail from his shadowed hideaway. It had been a while since any woman, human or Were, had garnered his attention the way this woman did.

A shift in the air—perhaps an anticipatory grin on her lovely face—something caught Lakon's attention. His brows furrowed as he watched her, flicking a brief look toward the booth she called to so casually.

"Okay, Myles," came her melodious voice. "Hit me!" She had an engaging, mild English accent.

Lakon's recorded voice stopped mid note, and the luxurious low tones of a saxophone began to play. The young girl grinned broadly and said, "Play Mr. Montgomery's song, sweet! The one that makes me think of him," she giggled.

The tune changed to the music of *"Smooth Operator"* by Sade and Mya raised her hands over her head and sang the first verse and chorus. Her hips swayed sensuously and Lakon watched, mesmerized.

"That was magic, luvie!" the girl smiled up at the box. "I feel recharged. Let's get back to work."

Lakon's most popular song filled the air again, and replaced Myles moving saxophone solo. She danced around the stage calling out colors again and pointing. As she did, the spotlights of color swept her slender body.

Finally, they heard Myles's voice boom from overhead.

"Come, let's away to prison; We two alone will sing like birds I' th' cage."

The tinkling sounds of the girl's laughter echoed in surround sound as she responded to Myles's King Lear quote.

"*As You Like It*, my love. Now go we in content, to liberty, and not to banishment," she quoted back to him as she stood shielding her eyes with an open palm, looking up at his booth.

"Right in one, Pet. Now, let's get thee to a Pub, shall we? We'll finish off tomorrow night."

Still laughing, she swept a low, exaggerated curtsey and made her way off the stage as all the lights went off. Lakon had recognized the finely formed beauty and her curved derriere from the day before. He and Yancey exchanged a meaningful glance, but otherwise sat silently, waiting to see what would happen next.

They heard the squeak of stairs and then a click, and finally watched as a young, dark haired man came through a doorway beneath the lighting and sound box, his form outlined under a muted light. In one hand he carried what Lakon realized was a saxophone in its black case. His free hand reached for the girl's as the two headed for the main doors leading out of the auditorium.

"I could fair murder a kebab and a plate of chips," they heard the man say.

As the couple left the building, they called a greeting and goodbye to the security guard before the echo of the heavy doors closing sounded through the large room.

Lakon turned to Yancey.

"That was definitely entertaining," he stated blandly. "Why haven't I seen those two before?"

"I thought you saw them when we were setting up in Virginia the other day? In fact, I know you did. Well, usually they only come out at night, Lake. Maybe it's easier to work with the lights at night." Yancey thought about this a minute. "They don't mix a lot with others—especially the girl. Myles keeps his distance, too, though."

"They're not Vamps are they?" Lakon asked in alarm. He didn't mind working with Vampires but he did like to know when they were around.

"No, of course not! I would have run it by you before I hired a vampire, you know that." Yancey sounded a little hurt that Lakon would question his common sense.

"Stop acting like an old woman, Yance, it was a fair question," he laughed at his cousin.

"Humph," Yancey conceded. Lakon's chuckle died away as his eyes began to narrow.

"If they purposefully avoid others, they're hiding something. Find out what you can. Let's do this again tomorrow."

"They've been working for you at least a year now, Lake. Why bother them now?" Yancey asked, eyes narrowed.

Lakon turned his head. He didn't' want his cousin to see the uncertainty he knew would show on his face. *Why bother them now?* That was a good point.

"I'm interested and they work for me," he said finally. It would have to do.

* * * *

Once again, the werewolves stood outside the auditorium for a minute talking.

"Okay, what did you find out?" Lakon asked his cousin quietly.

"Not a whole lot, to be honest. They've been with us longer than I thought. About two years or so, as best I can tell. Before that, they moved from job to job – not staying in one place for long," Yancey's voice sounded puzzled. "Everything I *did* to find out about them met with a dead end. I've got some feelers out, but I don't expect anything. They're English, so it's not going to be easy."

"I'm pretty sure they're not dangerous, Yancey, but my curiosity is piqued. Let's go in and watch tonight's performance." Lakon gave his cousin a devious smile. "I can't wait to see what they do next."

Once inside, Lakon and Yancey moved to the gloomy recesses of the hall and sat down. As they watched, Mya once again called out light colors as recordings of Lakon's songs played.

Finally Lakon's recorded voice stopped. Both men were stunned by what happened next.

"Okay, darling, work's over. Let's play!" That was Myles's rich, accented voice from overhead. Its smooth timbre echoed throughout the auditorium.

"Myles are you *sure* there's nobody here? I'd hate to get caught!" This came from Mya who was speaking into the microphone on stage. Her voice dropped to a nervous murmur. "When he's mad, Mr. Brooks is a bit...off putting, y'know? I'd hate to make him angry."

Lakon enjoyed the hint of a British accent in her husky, melodic voice. He wondered what they were up to. He and Yancey exchanged looks.

"Halloo!" called Myles. "Halloo!" he called again. "See, luv, the coast is clear. Now, break my heart!"

Music began to play from overhead. It wasn't very loud so the men could clearly hear the voice that began with it. Mya had a smile on her face.

"Come on, pet, *hurt* me!" Myles called.

As the hidden audience sat in the shadows, Mya closed her eyes and began to sing. A beautiful and powerful female voice swelled and ebbed around them. The singer's emotions filled every corner of the arena.

Lakon was amazed at the skill and range Mya managed as her rich, soulful voice reached the song's crescendo and then eased her listeners through to the end. He started to step forward until Yancey laid a hand on his arm.

"Wait, cousin,.." Yancey whispered, not taking his eyes off the woman. Lakon saw him swipe at his eye and hid a smile. Yancey was pretty sensitive. "I don't think they're done yet."

"Thank you, darling," Myles asked over the loud speakers. "One more? I promise I'll feed you after."

The men heard Mya chuckle. "Only one more. Oh, and I have a new melody for Mr. M. that I want you to pass on."

"Yeah? Sure it's his speed?" he asked. "It's fair dodgy getting it to him."

"I'm sure. It's about Himself thinking with his goolies."

Myles let out a bark of laughter. "Goolies, huh? You didn't actually refer to his testicles directly did you? I'm sure it's a very clever song."

"Any idea what that meant?" Lakon asked Yancey.

"None whatsoever," came Yancey's answer.

"Okay, what'll ya have, then?" the girl asked her brother.

"Do that Dolly Parton song that Whitney Houston recorded," Myles requested.

"I will, if you'll play for me," she countered.

They were treated to two minutes of sensuous saxophone music as the girl swayed in rhythm on stage. Lakon couldn't take his eyes off of her. When it ended, she moaned.

"Mmm, oh, Myles," she sighed. "I love to listen to you play. Okay," she told him; the moment had passed.

He adjusted the music and Mya began singing *"I Will Always Love You"*.

The young lady was truly gifted. Both werewolves wondered why she kept her voice hidden away, not to mention *how*. Lakon decided to end that tonight. He'd become bored with his own voice and his own shows. He wanted to shake things up a bit. This lovely little thing would do nicely. It couldn't hurt her either, now, could it?

"You go north," he whispered to Yancey, pointing at the booth on the ceiling. "I'll go south," he said pointing at Mya. "I don't care if she *is* human—I want that girl to sing with us."

Yancey shrugged and gave a nod of agreement before heading in the direction opposite the way that Lakon had gone.

Chapter 2

Mya Brooks sat shivering next to her brother, Myles, as she watched Lakon Montgomery pace in front of her. Never had she expected to find herself in the famous singer's dressing room. The angry, *intimidating,* famous singer's dressing room. She was trying to listen but she was definitely very shaken. Myles wrapped an arm about her shoulders and gave her a squeeze. Their boss arched a brow but said nothing.

The man who'd hired them two years before, Yancey Livingston, presented the offer to the siblings. Mya would sing one song alone at each concert and one or two duets with Lakon. She'd be paid and given plenty of time to prepare. She could still work with her brother if she chose.

Myles could be nearby or could continue to stay in the booth on the ceiling during concerts. He would accompany her on the saxophone whenever appropriate. In future, they would both travel with the band instead of the crew. Their position would be more permanent. Mya ground her teeth but said nothing. She'd felt safe when, after their hiring, Yancey had left them alone to work with the crew. So much for *that.*

After listening to Yancey's proposal, Myles asked if he could have a minute to talk to his sister. The two men graciously offered to leave the room for them. After they left, Myles turned to Mya.

"I'm so sorry, darling," he said. "I guess it was bound to happen."

"It's me, Myles. I don't know why I thought working with entertainers would suit us. We were certain to be found out," the girl sniffed. "I just figured we'd blend in and nobody would... well, doesn't matter, does it?"

"Don't worry, sweet, we'll get out of this somehow," Myles promised.

"I just...Are you sure? He's really...he's very big, isn't he? And sure of himself, too. I don't think he'll just let us go, you know? Does he sound a bit growly to you?"

"He's been taken by surprise, Mya-luv, that's all. As soon as he knows we've got issues, he'll forget about us, I'm certain."

* * * *

Mya hadn't known that the two men who had left the room so she could speak privately would hear every word just as clearly from the hall.

Eavesdropping shamelessly, Lakon and Yancey looked at each other in confusion. They were so used to people trying to break into their business that it was unusual to meet a talented singer who didn't want to sing professionally. They tuned back into the conversation— not that they'd really ever stopped listening.

"What do you think they will do when we tell them about the contract, Myles?" Mya asked. "We have to be honest with Mr. Montgomery."

Contract? Great! Just Great!

"We were children when that contract was signed, pet. I'm sure Himself can get us out of it. Maybe this is what we need." Myles sounded carefully hopeful. "You haven't sung a note professionally in nearly ten years and not once on this continent."

You can't sign children to a contract...their parents, sure, but children?

She must have seemed dubious because Myles added, "If he wants us, we're quids-in. If he doesn't, we'll just move on."

Mya's voice was choked with tears. "Myles, you need medical care, we can't keep moving on," she sniffled. "Myles... Do you think...? Would Mr. Montgomery... He's so big. He's a little scary, Myles," she said diffidently. "I don't want to fight him off, y'know?"

Lakon's eyes flashed green in the hallway. Rustling could be heard in the other room.

"Don't fret, luv," Lakon heard Myles kiss his sister. "I know Mr. M has a temper but I've never heard of him striking an employee. Or anything else, come to that. That sort of news gets around fast."

"Myles, I don't like to be around people. I make them mad," Mya's voice broke. "And I..."

"Hush, pet," he soothed. "You don't make people mad. Mad people act badly to you. We'll tell Mr. Montgomery that he can't hit you, okay?"

In the hallway, Lakon's eyes glowed steadily green and his teeth lengthened. He was having a real problem with anger management listening to the siblings talking. The werewolf snarled deep in his throat not sure if he was angry on his own behalf or angry because obviously, the young woman had been hurt as a child and possibly more recently. Yancey pulled him down the hall a few feet.

"Get a grip, Lake. She doesn't know you from Adam. We'll find out what's going on and see if we can fix it," Yancey growled back at him, calming him.

After a few more mumbled reassurances, Myles asked his sister, "Do you think we should say yes or hit the road, Mya? You're the one who'd have to do the work."

"If Mr. Montgomery can help us get free of Mother and Father and help us get your medicine..." She took a deep breath. "I'll do it. But I like singing best if you back me up. Do you agree?"

Apparently, he did agree because he opened the door. After a minute, Yancey and Lakon returned to the dressing room. Brother and sister received them apprehensively.

"We should tell you," began Myles without preamble, "back in England, when we were eight, our parents signed us to a contract." He squeezed his sister's hand.

"The contract said that Myles and I were the creative property of our parents and any money we generated through performing would go to them." Mya didn't look at anyone in the room. "They'd reimburse us as they saw fit."

"We ran away when we were fifteen," Myles told them. "Neither of us has performed in eight years. I have a copy of the contract in my room," he told them. "If you help dissolve that contract and cover our medical costs, Mya will perform for you."

"Myles!" she whispered. "I want you, too. And tell them the rest."

Lakon moved to stand in front of her. Her scent teased his nostrils. He stepped back a half pace.

"*You* tell me, Miss Brooks," he growled.

She flinched and didn't look up at him. Reaching for her brother's hand, she spoke barely above a whisper.

"When we left, we shut our parents in the loo and nicked 'em light," she said in a rush.

Myles' laugh was slightly vengeful. "Light, pet? We snatched 'em blind." Seeing the confusion on the faces of the other two, Myles explained, "We locked them in the bathroom and took every bit of money or jewelry we could find." Remembering the event fondly, Myles nudged his sister.

"We left Sid Vicious playing in the hall when we went off, didn't we, luv? A right nice screaming headache for every bruise on your lovely body," he snickered meanly. She laughed with him, a hint of remembered vengeance in her eyes.

Lakon turned his back to the siblings. He was having trouble controlling his beast. He was sure it was because the idea of parents abusing their children didn't sit right with him at all.

How could they laugh about her being bruised? Why her and not him, too?

"Bring the contract to me tomorrow, Myles," Yancey told him. "It should be a simple matter to nullify it."

With his back to them, Lakon said, "Go get some rest. I'll let you know when and what I want to practice. You can leave the new song with Yancey tomorrow, too." He walked to the door, pausing and looked back over his shoulder. "I want you to play for me as well, Mr. Brooks, make no mistake. Your talent won't be wasted." With a sharp nod, he walked away.

Chapter 3

Around noon the next day, Myles made his way to Yancey Livingston's hotel room atop the inn. He was nervous, but the other man politely welcomed him into his suite and offered him a drink. Myles gratefully accepted a cup of tea and the two men sat down.

"Let's have a look at that contract, Mr. Brooks. You do know that I'm a lawyer, don't you? I handle all of Lakon's contracts and legal obligations."

Myles studied him closely and decided that things could only improve. Certainly, it would be nice to be free of the oppressive contract their parents had forced on his sister and himself. He extended the contract to his boss's manager. Yancey took the folded papers from the younger man and spread them out across a small table.

"Please, Mr. Livingston, I think you're the elder here. Call me Myles," he said, trying to show respect.

"You know most people don't like being reminded of their age, Myles," Yancey laughed. "Well, would you look at this…?" The manager began to read the contract with interest.

Myles sat back and enjoyed his tea. It wasn't the best he'd ever had, nor was it the worst. It was a very nice gesture from the older man. He could tell that Yancey was lost to him for a few minutes. He watched the shifting emotions on his host's face. That contract must be very creative, indeed.

"Okay, young man…" Yancey began, drumming his fingers on the table. "Here's what we've got…"

Yancey's brows knit again and he looked off into space. Myles felt sure he'd arrive at a point eventually. It was probably best to let him get to it in his own time.

"Okay…" Yancey started again.

Myles tried hard to control the smile playing about his mouth. In fact, he had to turn his head to hide his grin in response to Yancey's fixations. When he did, he looked into the eyes of Lakon Montgomery who entered from another room. The other man had been so quiet he hadn't even noticed his arrival.

Lakon was wearing a brief pair of denim cutoff shorts. Myles had time to consider what a handsome brute the blond man was before Lakon joined him at the table.

"Hey, Brooks," he said, slapping the younger man's left shoulder.

With difficulty, the young man hid a wince. *He doesn't know his own strength.* He clenched his teeth and tightened his muscles, hoping the stinging, prickling feeling wasn't the beginning of something much worse than a simple contusion.

Myles suffered from a form of Hemophilia and hadn't had any clotting factor treatments in a while. Although Lakon hadn't hit him hard, he knew there'd be a bruise. He hoped it wouldn't be more than that, though the blow had been quite near his shoulder. Joints tended to be more sensitive for him.

He managed to greet Lakon casually enough and both men turned to Yancey again. He wasn't sure how he felt about the newcomer, to be honest. Stealing a look at his boss, Myles knew why his sister was especially afraid of Lakon Montgomery. He was huge, muscular, and overwhelmingly male. He had dark blond hair interspersed with a hint of salt and pepper. Instead of causing him to look older, it made him look more masculine. He knew the man was within ten years of his and Mya's age. Those mesmerizing green eyes just enhanced his intense good looks.

Myles worked out and was muscular in his own right. He wasn't nearly as tall or broad as Lakon Montgomery was, though.

"Alright, Yance quit messing around," the larger man growled. "What's up with that contract?"

After a minute, Yancey answered, "It's artfully done, Lake." He shook his head. "I'll have to check out British Law, we may want to hire someone. Looks like anything that Myles and Mya have done to generate income up until their majority – legally, the proceeds of that work belong to their parents. *Anything.*"

Both Myles and Lakon were dumbstruck.

"So…" Myles began. "The time Mya worked as a waitress in that truck-stop when she was sixteen – every penny she earned legally goes to them?" he asked. Yancey nodded. "My job cleaning portable toilets? They get the money?" Yancey winced, but nodded.

"That's amazing," he shook his head. "But wait a second! Aren't they responsible for our health care during that time frame?" Myles hoped they were.

"Sorry, Pal," He really did look sorry. "Seems they were only responsible for your health care if you lived under their roof."

Myles groaned. "So we have to figure out how much we made and send it to them?"

"'Fraid so. At least…" Yancey looked at Lakon.

"What?" barked Lakon.

"If you two continue to hide out, it's up to your parents to find you and force you to pay up. If you two go public, then …" Yancey left the rest unsaid.

"So, let me get this straight," Lakon began to pace. "If they go public, the parents will come and we need to pay 'em, right?" Yancey nodded. "What if these two go public and we make *them* push the issue? They'd still have to take 'em to court." Lakon glared at Yancey and Myles.

"That's fine, Lake, but the publicity would be almost as nasty as having to go through all that."

"Yance, it would look worse for them than for us. Assholes treating their kids like machinery!" he spat. "And how is it possible to hold two minors to a contract they didn't even sign in a different country?" he demanded.

Yancey studied the document for a few more minutes.

"I *told* you we'd need to seek advice from a British lawyer. What do they call them? Solicitors, right? Doesn't matter, from what I can tell, this can be broken at their majority. How long you worked for us, Brooks?" Yancey asked.

"About two years, sir." Myles answered him, trying to remain polite and aware of the boundaries between them. The fact that one of the men was barely dressed and the other was…well, confusing at best, he was struggling with his manners just a bit.

"I'm not that damned much older than you, boy," growled Yancey. They all laughed.

"Okay, for now, we need to worry about buying them out of the last…" Yancey peered at Myles. "How old are you two?"

"Twenty-three," Myles answered.

"Then it's only a few years. Let's go talk to your sister and see what she wants to do." Yancey stood.

"Mr. Livingston, Yancey, we don't have the money to buy them out even for six years," Myles shook his head sadly. "And I'm pretty sure there's the matter of a green card…"

Lakon spoke up, "We'll add buying out your previous contract as part of the deal, Brooks," Lakon growled. "I take it personally when adults jerk kids around. I think between us, the green card can be taken care of, too. Let's go see your sister."

"Let me go in first, gents, and have a word. She's a bit skittish," Myles explained a little awkwardly. "You're a bit intimidating," he said carefully, making sure that Lakon knew that *he* was the more daunting of the two.

The three men stood up and headed down to Myles and Mya's mini-suite.

* * * *

Myles let the two men into the suite behind him and bade them to wait while he went to find his sister. He appreciated that the boss allotted certain number of suites for the crew. Many of them were used to being together and sharing space. Myles and Mya always made sure they stayed together, even if in the same room.

When she heard the door open, Mya called out, "Myles you've got to see this!"

Myles smiled apologetically and walked to one of the two rooms off the small sitting area.

"Hey, luvie..." she turned to face him. "Bloody hell!" she spat, no doubt alarming the two men in the other room. He had known she would notice the pain behind his eyes. She was far too used to looking for it. The way they'd lived their lives thus far, it was just part of the day for them, for her to watch him for injuries, just as he watched her for the stress of unwanted attention.

"Where is it, Myles, what happened?"

He'd never be able to hold Mya off if she thought he was injured. It simply wasn't possible. After a few moments of consideration, Myles turned away, hoping she'd follow him deeper into the room and present less entertainment for the two men waiting for them.

"Mr. Livingston looked at our contact with the parents, pet," he began. "He thinks it's possible to break it, one way or two. You're going to have to..." Mya held up one small hand, palm out and glared at him.

"Stop right there and answer me!"

Following the voices, Lakon saw her through the open door as she placed both hands on her slim hips in an angry demand. When her brother didn't respond, she drew herself up to her full five feet and some-odd inches.

"If you don't come clean right now, I'm going to go out and snog the first big, hairy bloke I come across!" she threatened.

"Since that big, hairy bloke is likely to be our boss, I guess I'll come clean," Myles laughed with a grimace.

The two men in the other room edged closer to the door to what could only be Mya's bedroom.

"What does snog mean?" Lakon asked Yancey in a whisper. If he was going to get snogged, he wanted to be aware when it happened.

"I think it means to kiss. Um, I'll check," Yancey promised Lakon, never taking his eyes away from the two.

Mya leaned forward a little, edging into her brother's personal space. The young woman was wearing a ripped pair of old jeans and a threadbare flannel shirt held together by one barely there button and Lakon couldn't believe how badly he hoped the beleaguered thread holding it in place would give up its battle.

His dishonorable intent toward her button was forgotten when Myles unfastened his own shirt and let it fall, turning his left shoulder toward his sister and the door.

As the young man turned, both Yancey and Lakon got a good look at the dark and angry purple bruise clearly outlined on his shoulder. Remembering his greeting to the younger man less than an hour ago, he had no doubt that his hand would fit that bruise perfectly.

Mya climbed up on the bed and standing, lightly skimmed the tips of her fingers over the injury.

"How'd it happen, sweet?" she asked.

"It was a "hail fellow, well met" tap, luv. No harm meant." He sat down on the corner of the mattress as she knelt behind him and kissed his shoulder.

"Myles, it could be bleeding inside. How much money do we have?"

Not waiting for an answer, Mya scrambled off the bed and bent over, pulling a battered suitcase from underneath. The view afforded the men in the doorway of her unfettered breasts gave Lakon an instant hard-on. He had to fight not to push Yancey aside to prevent his looking.

"Okay, we have enough money for an emergency room visit and at least one transfusion." She appeared to be thinking hard and then said, "I think we can pay full price for a clotting factor. But just one for now."

Still seated on the bed, Myles dropped his head to his hands. Mya rested her head on his knee.

"Myles, I can raise more money if I have to. I can do it again. You know I can." Her voice had no inflection.

"I'd rather die, Mya," he responded. It was apparent that he'd forgotten Yancey and Lakon in the other room. He rested a hand on her head.

"You know I won't let you," he whispered to his sister.

"Your medical costs are covered, Brooks," he ground out, surprising the siblings badly. "Did I cause that to happen?" Lakon didn't wait for an answer.

Mya, who had been sitting on the floor resting against her brother, jerked with a start and scrambled to her feet at the sound of Lakon's voice.

"Yancey, take him to the closest hospital. My cousin Jesse is a doctor on staff at Temple...This is Pennsylvania, isn't it?" he didn't wait for an answer. "I'll call you in the car." He turned to look at Mya. "Go with your brother. Yancey will bring you back."

With that, Lakon walked out of the room. He didn't know what she meant to do to raise the money but he had his suspicions. Just the thought of her near other men made his beast snarl and threaten to break free.

Chapter 4

Rehearsals
Wachovia Center
Philadelphia, Pa

Myles was healing well by the next day, though he was taking it much easier. Yancey had called ahead from the car, and the trio had been met right away in the emergency room. Myles had been seen immediately and treated with a clotting factor infusion with a series scheduled both at that particular hospital and at a doctor's office on their next stop.

Mya and Lakon were currently seated on stage facing one another and rehearsing together. Things seemed to be going well until Lakon reached out to touch her. He'd been trying to avoid her scent but she smelled so good.

Mya flinched back and Lakon had to fight for control. He broke off his rehearsal with her and had her begin to practice a song on her own. It was time to talk to her brother.

Finding Myles was the easy part. Getting him to talk was not as easy. Finally, Lakon let his frustration show.

"Damn it man!" he growled at Myles. "How are we going to get to know each other and do anything together if she's scared to death of me?"

Myles stared at him speculatively for a minute.

"Do you really care if my sister is afraid?" he asked finally.

"What the hell kind of question is that?" Lakon barked back.

Myles continued to regard him steadily.

"I'll talk to her. She'll be much better when you go live," he finally told his boss and began to turn away.

"What the hell is *that* supposed to mean? I don't just want her to perform better, Myles. I want her to *be* better," Lakon said softly; his voice had a threatening edge to it. "You tell me why she's afraid. Don't give me any shit about stage fright or nerves, either," he growled.

Myles breathed a heavy sigh. "She's afraid of men, one on one. I'm her twin so I don't count. Our father hurt her. He liked to hit her. He never tried to touch her sexually, though."

After a minute, Myles stood and turned to the window.

"There's more."

"Talk," Lakon growled menacingly, his eyes narrowed and fixed on the young man. Myles obviously considered what he wanted to say, or possibly whether to speak at all, Lakon couldn't be sure.

"We'd been in the states almost two years when I got hurt. She wouldn't tell me how she paid the hospital or chemist, but I know. The head surgeon was a right bloater – a fat oaf – and he had an eye for her. A real sadist that one."

Lakon had to turn away. Even now he could see and hear her as she sang on stage. She'd calmed down now that he'd moved away and was laughing happily with one of the band members. The idea of anybody hurting that small and beautiful woman ate into his gut. He felt his teeth lengthen and his claws begin to extend. With difficulty, he forced his beast to recede. Going primal wouldn't help anyone just now.

Although his intention had always been to keep his distance from that beautiful human female, it was becoming harder and harder. *Hell, who was he trying to fool? He couldn't stay away from her and didn't really want to.*

Her scent drew him in. Hunger for her gnawed his insides. An ache to touch her grew in him every minute he spent with her. The more he was around Mya the more he needed to be closer. He longed to hold her and feel her against him.

In a flash of empathy, he understood Riker's need to hold his mate even when she was ill. He'd thought it was simply because they had been so long apart that Riker had insisted on doing so many things for Bethany, on holding her as she slept, ill and dead to the world.

Lakon wanted to sit quietly with Mya on his lap. His arms ached to be around her when she watched a movie or read a book. He even longed to feel his thighs bump against hers when sitting next to her.

That thought brought him up short. *Was that frail human with the voice of an angel his mate? How could that be? He'd never even touched her. How would he know?* Lakon decided that he might need to call his Dad right away.

He had to make peace with these feelings because as hard as his beast was to control when he imagined her in pain, the predator inside of him was impossible to handle when he imagined life without her.

He didn't know how it had happened, but he needed this woman. Few knew of the violence and anger he kept under lock and key deep inside himself. Deceptively, he had a jovial façade, but that mask hid a snarling animal rigidly contained. If he didn't keep this woman in his life, he would be even more dangerous than he was already. Nobody would be safe.

Lakon rested a hand on Myles's shoulder, overwhelmed by a sudden, unexpected insight. He thought he understood the younger man's pain. Even if he didn't understand it completely, he empathized.

"I'm a twin," he told Myles. "I can't think of anything I wouldn't do for my brother. *Anything,*" he emphasized. Carefully, he gave Myles' shoulder a little rub, not daring to squeeze after the last days' experience, and walked out.

Lakon went to his dressing room and called his father.

Armed with his new awareness and renewed determination, Lakon worked hard to be more understanding when he and Mya sang together. He found himself divided between frustration at not being able to touch her as freely as he wanted, or at all, frankly, and anger at the events and people to blame for her wariness.

* * * *

Leaning back into the plush theater chair and closing her eyes, Mya lost herself in the soothing sound of her brother's music. The stadium was empty and rich melody filled the air. There was nothing quite like the full, fluid sound of the saxophone to carry her away. Nobody could move her quite like her brother when he played.

She felt her heart gallop as the sound swelled and then drifted smoothly down, calming her as it eased her through to the end. Tears in her eyes, she sniffled, chuckling at herself.

"What is it, pet?" Myles asked, lowering his instrument and looking at her quizzically.

"'s nothing, My," she assured him, though he didn't appear convinced when she scrubbed at an errant tear. "No, really, it's just when you play from your heart like that, it always gets me."

A faint pink tint highlighted Myles' cheeks. "What a lovely thing to say, beautiful sister. So, did you just come to compliment me, or was there something else?"

He knew her so well. "Yeah, I did want to talk." She glanced sideways at him as he settled in the chair next to hers. As stadium seating went, this was nicer than most of her recollection.

"At your service, pet."

Squirming self consciously, she took a deep breath. "It's Mr. Montgomery. He makes me uncomfortable," she blurted.

Her brother tensed beside her. "In what way," he asked carefully, his voice tight.

"Uh, well…" Mya struggled to find just the right words. She knew she'd made Myles think that their boss had done something inappropriate and that wasn't so. "I'm sorry, My, I didn't mean he'd done anything wrong. It's just…I kind of like him but I sort of feel squirmy around him. Sweaty and a bit dreadful, you know? And then…well, he *is* a mite gruff, isn't he?"

Staring straight ahead, Myles appeared to be thinking deeply. They were close enough she knew he'd understand what she was trying to convey.

"You have a crush on Himself then, do you?"

"Do I?" she murmured softly.

"All signs indicate that, yeah," he confirmed.

"You sound like one of those eight ball toys!"

"Wisdom is wisdom, pet, even if it's written in cheap plastic."

She elbowed him sharply, though not too sharply, which led to him pulling her hair. A brief, muted scuffle ensued ending in him lifting the arm between their seats so that she could lean against him.

Sighing heavily, she continued her conversation. "Well what am I going to do about it, Myles? I don't know how to have a real relationship with a guy, or even if I want to." She paused. "And then, he's scary, like I said. I'm nervous and jumpy around him. I don't know how not to be. Except, I *do* want to be around him. I can't seem to help it. What do I do?" There was a distinct whine to her voice, she couldn't deny that. But the entire situation was so frustrating.

Myles sighed gustily, his warm breath teasing her hair. "I'm not saying I'm chuffed about it, Mya, but it's quite all right to have a crush on 'im. He's a sexy beast, innit'e?"

Mya snickered and then snorted. "Somehow, that's actually spot on, big brother." After a calming second or two, she went on. "He does put one in mind of a ravening beast, doesn't he? Or a sexy predator. Makes you want to pet him, even when you know he's gonna bite you."

"Or eat you up, hmm?" Myles teased knowingly. "You're a big girl, luv. I'm always there for you, any way you let me, but you have to work some things out for yourself." Pulling back, he cast a sly glance. "You're a bit of a saucy minx yourself. I think you can handle the brute."

The narrowing of her eyes was enough to send him shimmying out from under her comfortable embrace. Mya was right behind him, shrieking and sputtering as she chased him up the stairs to the stage.

It felt good to be so carefree and childish with her brother. It was more than a little reassuring to know that he supported her in this uncertain foray into possible romance. While he hadn't put it in quite those terms, Myles' meaning had been pretty clear to her. *You're old enough to have a libido and to use it. Make a decision and follow it through.*

Assuming the interest went both ways and she could overcome her fears and insecurities, maybe she *would* see this through. It was just possible that Lakon Montgomery was more than she could handle, but she didn't really want anyone else.

* * * *

Though Lakon didn't intend to have her perform with him during the first few concerts at the current venue, he hoped to have her ready by the end of their sojourn there. There was also the issue of the sound and lighting crew that would be needed to replace Mya and Myles.

It wasn't surprising that Myles insisted on carrying out his old duties in addition to performing with his sister. She, of course, didn't want him to have to do the work on his own, but was so exhausted from the extra rehearsals that working late at night was impossible. It was times like this that Lakon realized how far he'd come from his early days as a club singer and how far he really was from his crew, no matter what he liked to tell himself. With that in mind, he made an effort to work with Myles and the other man's replacement. Before long, he began to feel more a part the human, or werewolf, mechanism that made up each of his performances on tour. In addition, he got to know Myles and Mya a little better.

Lakon tried to made it a practice to have Mya take some of her meals with him each day since that first night. He hoped she'd relax with him if she got used to being around him.

The day of the final concert, Lakon and Mya rehearsed the duet they were to sing that night. When he reached for her near the end of the song, she flinched. Losing control, Lakon exploded at her.

"Good God, woman!" he shouted, frustration overwhelming him. "What do you think I'm going to do?"

Her eyes widened dramatically as she froze in fear for a moment, and then shot to her feet and dashed from the stage. Right that minute, Lakon didn't care who noticed them or what they thought. He sprang to his feet and charged after her. Halfway down the long hallway she'd dashed into, he heard a closet door slam and he sprinted toward it.

There was only the one door and it had no lock so he opened it and stepped in, closing it behind him. Her unbelievable scent filled the small room. He inhaled deeply. *Sugar and spice and everything nice...* He bent down and gently pulled her to her feet.

She stood quaking and cringing under his hands, backing away as much as possible in the small space. He pulled her to him and wrapped his arms around her.

"Holy hell, baby!" he swore, his voice low, quiet, burying his face in her hair. "I'm not going to hurt you, I promise," he soothed her, one hand rubbing circles on her back. Her trembling began to lessen somewhat.

He tilted her chin with one hand. There was only the thinnest strip of light to be seen in the darkened closet, but he could see quite well. From experience, he knew his eyes must appear to be glowing somewhat. Before he gave her a chance to think about that, he lowered his mouth to hers.

He licked her bottom lip. "Mmm," he groaned and licked her top lip. He slid one hand under her shirt at the back of her waist. The other hand he buried in her hair.

Lakon licked her lips again, whispering, "Open your mouth, Mya, let me taste you." She opened her mouth with a reluctant sigh.

His movements were slow and sensuous. His body stroked against hers as he traced her upper lip with his tongue again and nibbled at her generous lower lip. He moved his tongue across her teeth and between them. Their tongues mated sinuously as he slid his over hers.

With gentle fingertips, he massaged her scalp with the hand in her hair while the hand at the small of her back slipped lower. His questing fingers moved under the waist of her jeans and slipped into her panties to cup her bare bottom.

He continued to savor her sweet flavor as his wayward hand found its way between her legs. She gasped.

The hand in her hair caressed down the length of her neck and body to unfasten her jeans. He pushed them down with her panties and returned that hand to cup her head.

"Hush, baby," he murmured against her mouth swallowing her protests. "I'm going to show you how good my hands can make you feel. You never have to worry about me using them to hurt you."

He urged two fingers between her legs and stroked the wet heat he found there. He slid his fingers through the cream between her labia. Back and forth he moved his fingers rubbing against her small, engorged clit.

"Oh, Mr. Montgomery," she groaned.

Lakon chuckled. He kissed her again and pinched her little nub between his two fingers.

"Lakon, baby," he said. When she didn't respond, he pinched a little bit harder. "Call me Lakon," he growled.

She gasped. "L – La – Lakon," she moaned.

"That's it, honey," he growled. "That's my baby. Come for me, Mya," he ordered.

He plunged a finger inside of her. Pumping, he added a second one and before he knew it she was climaxing around his hand. As his fingers plunged, he could feel how tight she was. She hadn't been with anyone in a long time.

He removed the fingers from inside of her and automatically put them in his mouth. This drew a growl from deep inside of him.

Her smell, her taste, he was overwhelmed by her. He tightened his arms around her and buried his face in her hair. If he hadn't been trying to show her that she could trust him, he would have taken his pleasure with her right there in the closet.

He ran his hands over her naked bottom and tilted her head back for a long, lingering kiss. It took a great deal of willpower to lift his mouth away from her soft lips, but somehow he managed. For long moments, he held her close, her head resting against his hammering heart as it slowed. Once he'd calmed a bit, he pulled back to help her adjust her pants and put her clothing back together. Still nervous, she clutched his shirt before he could open the door.

"La – Lakon?" she whispered.

"It's okay, baby," he soothed. "You're okay," he purred, tilting her face up to his once again. He could get lost in those beautiful, brandy colored eyes. "I tried to stay away from you but I can't," he confessed. "You and I are going to get to know each other much better, Mya."

"I don't understand," she choked. "I'm not sure this is…right. I'm not that good at dealing with men. You're my boss, too. I should have…done something."

"Mya, are you afraid of me?" He still held her in his arms. He'd pulled her pants up and fastened them, and cuddled her against his body.

"Answer me, baby, are you afraid of me?" he growled at her. She began to shake.

"Mr. – I mean Lakon," she managed, clearing her throat. "I don't want to be afraid of you. It's just…"

"It's just what, Mya?" he asked her gently.

"Well." She took a deep breath. "You're scary," she rushed out.

He lowered his head and licked her temple.

"What makes me scary, baby?" he asked, nipping and licking at her cheek and pulling her closer. She giggled.

"I guess that makes you not as scary," she giggled again as he licked her ear. "Slightly gross, but not quite as scary."

"Maybe I should do more of that, then," he smiled, licking her behind the ear now. "Tell me what I do that *is* scary, baby," he asked again.

"You're very growly," she said finally. "Your voice is so deep and rough. It's a bit scary. I…I mean…"

"Let's get out of this closet and talk about this a little bit, hmmm?" he asked her.

He could tell she was still nervous, but not nearly as bad, and she nodded, so that was all the agreement he needed.

* * * *

Once they arrived in his dressing room, Lakon set about preparing a pot of coffee. While it perked, he showed her around his dressing room. It had a sizeable, well-lit mirror across one wall and a couch, an overstuffed chair and a coffee table taking up a large part of the room. There was a bathroom and a curtained off dressing area.

"The next place we stop, you will have your own dressing room," he told her.

"Why?" she asked. He rolled his eyes at her and shook his head in disbelief.

"What do you mean why? Don't you want a dressing room?" he asked and arched a brow at her.

31

"I can get dressed in the loo," she reasoned, sitting at the table. Lakon laughed out loud.

"All right, baby, we'll work that out later. I want to talk about how growly I am."

She shot to her feet again and paced away from him. Brows furrowed, she was clearly searching for the right words to express her thoughts. As far as he was concerned, there was no reason that she couldn't do that from much closer. He looped an arm around her waist and scooped her into his arms. He took three strides to the couch and dropped with her in his lap.

She began to struggle uncomfortably and he lowered his mouth to hers. "Shh, it's okay, it's just me and you," he murmured. "Only a kiss, that's all." As she began to reply, his tongue glided between her parted lips as he deepened his possession of her mouth.

Mya stilled in his arms as the kiss deepened. When air became an issue, he backed up enough to kiss her lightly and dipped in for another, and another. Finally, reluctantly, he lifted his mouth from hers and licked at her lips. He nuzzled her cheek and licked her temple.

"We have to talk about this, baby," he rumbled insistently.

She softened against him and turned her face to his neck. He could feel her tremble.

"Mya?" he asked, she nodded against him. "Do you know that I won't hurt you?"

For a long moment, she didn't move. Finally, she shrugged one slender shoulder against him. He smiled slightly and tightened his arms around her. They had the honesty thing going for them, anyway.

"I *won't* hurt you, baby. And I'll do everything I can to make sure nobody else does either, okay?" he held her away from him so he could see her face. "Do you understand?"

She nodded.

"About this growly thing…" he gave her a half-smile. "It's kind of a family trait. We're very… *primal,*" he grinned at her, wriggling his brows playfully. She blushed.

"I really can't help it too much," he said more seriously. "I'll try harder to be…well, more like rumbly instead of growly, okay?" he arched a brow at her.

"Okay," she said finally. He held her closer for a minute.

"Mya, I want to make love with you pretty badly right now." She stared at him, her eyes round. "I want to, baby, but I'll wait."

He kissed her gently, dipping his tongue between her lips in a quick taste, and licking her left dimple as he withdrew.

"Feel how badly I want you." He shifted so that she could feel his thick, hard erection under her soft bottom. "Do you think you might want me too, Mya?" he asked her.

"I think I do," she whispered, "But…"

"You're scared, baby?" he finished for her. She nodded.

"Let's go tease each other for a while. We'll sing to each other, hmm? Pretty soon we'll want each other too much to be scared or cautious, you think?"

Cheeks flaming, she slid off his lap. He stood, taking her hand and together, they returned to the rehearsal stage.

Chapter 5

"How'd you like that pretty lady?" Lakon asked the auditorium full of screaming fans after Mya left the stage. She'd just performed her first solo. He gave them a few minutes to settle down. Mya had been a big hit.

His voice dropped an octave. "Can I tell you guys something? Just between us?" he asked, waving a hand between himself and the audience, and waited until the crowd began responding in catcalls and shouts.

"Tell us!" and "We won't tell! We promise!"

"I'm kinda sweet on that girl, ya know?" he confessed, glancing over his shoulder toward the backstage hallway. The crowd broke into screams, cheering and shouting. "How 'bout if I get her back out here to sing a song with me?" The room exploded with more wild cheers and screaming. He grinned broadly.

"Why don't we all just call her?" he asked. He turned. "Hey, Mya! Will you come out and sing with me?" Lakon shouted, hands cupped around his mouth as if there were no microphones in sight.

The room exploded again and the fans began to chant, "Mya! Hey, Mya!"

A few minutes later, a very red-faced Mya came back out on stage. The spotlight shrunk to follow her as she joined him. When she reached him, it seemed to hold them intimately. Lakon ran one finger down her cheek.

"Sing a song with me, baby?" he rumbled as if it were only the two of them.

"Maybe," she teased. "Which song did you have in mind?"

"Hmm...What about that song we've been practicing on?"

"Okay, Lakon." She looked up at him through the fan of her lashes, her flirting causing his blood to simmer.

He looked into deeply into her eyes and she gazed back, both so totally focused upon one another that, to Lakon the room seemed to disappear. The song they sang to each other was one of intense longing and emotion and Lakon felt every word deeply. As the singers became lost in the moment, the auditorium became still and quiet. The audience was riveted as Lakon and Mya begged each other to give their love a chance.

When the last notes ebbed away, the hall remained still as seconds ticked by. Lost in the moment, Lakon leaned down and gently kissed Mya's parted lips, drawn as if by the magic of the moment. As he straightened, she leaned her head forward to rest it on his chest and he slipped his arms around her waist.

Suddenly, an incredible roar ripped through the building. Lakon and Mya had been so lost in each other that they'd forgotten the audience. He knew she was as embarrassed as he was. How could they forget about twenty thousand people all of a sudden?

Even with all the noise, the auditorium full of spectators heard Mya's sheepish comment to Lakon as the microphone amplified her voice above the crowd.

"I forgot everybody was out there," she said, her face stained red.

The fans loved it. Lakon loved it too, for different reasons. He was glad he wasn't the only one who'd been sucked into this new alternate universe. He had no doubt that newspaper and magazine reporters would never let them live it down. No doubt there would be fan interviews speculating about them and their relationship. At least this time, there really was a fire to go with all the smoke

* * * *

In the high security wing of the Livingston Care Facility August Livingston pelted the television bolted to the wall with his plastic cup full of tepid coffee followed immediately by a stale raspberry filled donut. He was purportedly enjoying the two hours of stimulation he was allowed every day in the facility's predominantly plastic and vinyl recreation room. He knew his little outburst would earn him a reprimand – possibly even cost him a privilege or two.

The very idea of it enraged him. His pretty-boy cousins were free to prance around the country as Alpha and Beta of the combined Livingston/Montgomery pack while he was locked up. Locked up in hell—otherwise known as Livingston's Long Term Care Facility for the Criminally Unstable, Johnston City, Tennessee location. It was Riker Montgomery's fault that he was in this *facility* to begin with. In fact, he blamed both Montgomery brothers' and if it was the last thing he ever did, Auggie would see to it that they suffered as much as he did for as long as possible, and *soon*.

Even though Riker and Lakon Montgomery were the Alpha and Beta of the joint Montgomery and Livingston pack, they weren't even pureblooded werewolves! That factor alone made Auggie crazy. They had *no* business running any pack but especially not such an enormous and intricate pack as this one. A pack as big as theirs called for a leader who could appreciate what being a werewolf really meant. Besides that, a large pack really needed someone with business acumen. Those two failed both requirements as far as Auggie was concerned.

Not only were the Montgomery brothers half timber wolf, or some kind of mundane wolf, anyway, but now Riker had mated with a human woman and had two pups with her.

As if that weren't enough, he was forced to watch Riker's brother, Lakon Montgomery, singing and kissing this new little human every time the TV came on. Lakon would mate with that full human, no werewolf in her bloodstream at all as far as Auggie could tell, however lovely she might be, and water down the family bloodline even more.

August just couldn't stand it. He was a full-blood werewolf, both his parents were full bloods. Mik Montgomery, who was Riker's and Lakon's father, couldn't even transform into the form of a man! It happened once every thousand or so births, especially when there was mixed blood in a family. As, of course, there was in that one. Now it looked like both Riker and Lakon would both be mating with humans. It was almost impossible to tell if Riker's pups had more wolf or more human in them, but they certainly weren't full werewolves.

Auggie remembered Bethany Montgomery. What a sweet little bite she'd been – the little taste that he'd had of her. One thing he could say for those Montgomery mongrels, they knew how to pick a hot-looking, sweet-smelling woman. *They're twins, this girl probably smells beautiful, too.*

He remembered touching, holding, licking Bethany Black Montgomery as her half-breed whelp looked on. *Now that had been a mouthful of good fun!* He'd been sure that Riker would kill him, but no, not heroic Riker. Any Alpha worth the name would have killed him for kidnapping his mate and pup.

He'd been so sure he'd take over the pack when Riker had gotten a human woman pregnant and hadn't told her he was Were. That's how it *should* have gone. August was second in line after Riker— well, Riker and Lakon, and the highest ranked of the family. He could have won a pack challenge, he was sure of it, especially if the challenge depended upon brains as much as brawn. That hadn't happened though, and now the other brother was mating with a human. Sure, the media had been known to spread unfounded rumors, but he could tell, just the way they were looking at each other. He wondered how much *she* knew about her new boyfriend.

"Auggie, you bad boy!"

Two large orderlies came up on either side of him, both placing a hand on his shoulder and pulling his other arm back behind him until they met. As he struggled and screamed in anger, the two men slipped a straightjacket around him and hauled him away, a smooth, well known, oft practiced dance. The entire routine made him so angry, he was sure his head would explode.

"I don't deserve this!" he roared. "I'm a full-blood! Lakon Montgomery shouldn't be allowed to mate with a human woman! He shouldn't be the co-Alpha, he shouldn't even be Beta!"

"I know man. My woman thinks he's hot, too. She goes nuts whenever she sees him. Now look, he's got that sweet little angel singing with him." That was a third orderly who stopped in the hall.

"Now don't encourage him, Joel. You see how he gets. We all hate how pretty and lucky that bastard is, but that's part of what makes him a good leader…"

Now Auggie had to listen to *three* men commiserate about Lakon Montgomery while he cooled his heels in a straight jacket. *If it kills me, I'll make those Montgomery mutts pay!*

Chapter 6

"Hello lovely little sister." Slipping his arms around Mya's waist, Myles held her tight as he blew a loud raspberry into her well coiffed hair.

"*My*-les!" she squealed, twisting away from him. "How did you sneak up on me, anyway? With me standing right in front of a mirror, you'd think I would have noticed," she groused. He leaned back and smirked, watching her carry on the conversation without him. "I'm getting ready for supper with Lakon, you know!" she scolded him. "I want to look nice and now I've got to start over. He'll be here at half seven and it's already half six!"

Myles snickered at her, earning a fierce glare. "Come on luv," he teased. "It's never taken you an hour to brush your hair before. Has Lakon done something to it?" He moved up behind her and relieved her of the brush. Drawing it through her long tresses, he went on. "You two are spending quite a bit of time together then, hmm? Things getting serious?"

"I-I think I'm…I'm pretty sure I'm falling for him. Really falling, not just sort of. No more crush. I can picture being old with him. You're not mad are you, Myles?" she asked, slightly breathlessly. He should have known she'd feel bad and worry for him. His sweet sister was all heart. "I've abandoned you, haven't I?"

Myles stepped back to admire his work and then lifted a bottle of smoother, squirting a little into his palm and then fluffing it through her hair. "Of course not, pet. I think it's a good thing that you've gotten yourself a bloke, truly. I do miss you a bit, but I'm pleased for you. Yancey and I are turning into right mates and that's just fine, too."

Her sigh of relief brought a small smile to his lips. She really was far too sensitive sometimes, though it warmed him that she worried for his feelings.

"Any little chickies on your horizon then, My?" she asked, tilting her head one way and then the other. "I like it," she declared, spinning to kiss his cheek.

"P'raps I should have been a hairdresser?" he quipped.

After wrinkling her nose at him, Mya leaned back and considered him seriously. "Are you sure you're okay with it being Himself though? And don't think I didn't notice you dodging my question."

Rolling his eyes in exasperation, Myles took his sister by the shoulders and gave her a firm shake. "I said it and I mean it, pet. I'm quite all right with you going out with the big man as long as he treats you as he should—which is good as gold. Should he ever stray from that path, I'll have to take him aside and show him what's what. Any good brother would."

She grinned and hugged him briefly. "And you're the best, of course…"

"Of course," he agreed. "Years of practice. As for a bird of my own, no. I'm quite discerning, as you know," he stated primly, lifting his chin resolutely. The effect was completely ruined when he waggled his eyebrows and added, "She's gotta be a sure thing…"

Mya huffed at him and stomped out of the small room, leaving Myles to trail behind her. "You know you don't mean that. Do you want a drink or a tea?" she called over her shoulder. Clearly, she had something more on her mind.

"Tea sounds fine. I'll likely be drinking later if Yancey and I do anything." He sat quietly and watched her fumble with the electric kettle and the tea pot. No doubt the familiar chore would help her organize her thoughts. "What's on your mind, luv?" he asked finally as the tea steeped and Mya continued to stand with her back to him. He was beginning to worry when another minute passed she failed to respond. "Mya?"

She cleared her throat. "I-this is difficult, My," she managed, her voice raspy.

"Take your time, pet, but be aware that I'm getting quite nervous…"

Fine china rattled musically as she placed cups, saucer and teapot along with sugar and milk on a small tray and carried it into the adjacent sitting room. It was a small suite that the two shared with a tiny kitchenette, two bedrooms and a cozy conversation area. Myles liked it far better than anywhere they'd stayed over the years. It was almost like a little apartment. They were certainly moving up in the world.

Seated across from him, Mya poured the tea and prepared her own cup. Without looking up, she finally spoke.

"I want to have sex, Myles."

Spewing tea and choking, Myles somehow managed to place his cup back onto the low table without scalding himself. "Sodding hell, woman! Warn a bloke will you?" he wheezed, coughing and sputtering as Mya pounded his back.

"Well, you wanted to know! But, sorry about that. You better now?"

Myles cleared his throat and nodded, leaning forward to mop up his spilled tea. "So." He cleared his throat again, trying to rid himself of the errant tea that he'd sucked into his esophagus at Mya's guileless announcement. "Uh, are you asking me or telling me about your sex life?"

"Heaven's sake! Telling! Talking!" she snapped. Heaving a breathy sigh, she tried again. "I need some advice, My. And I'm nervous, you know?"

He took a deep breath and studied his sister. She'd been through so much over the years. There were times he'd despaired of either one of them ever living anything that qualified as a normal life.

Myles didn't answer for long moments, holding up one hand to stop his sister from speaking as he calmed down and sipped at his tea. Frankly, he *really* didn't want to be having this conversation with his baby sister, but who else did she have to talk to?

"All right," he said finally. "Let's start again. I'll recap, shall I? As I understand it, you feel strongly about Lakon, yes?" Mya nodded. "You're ready to take your relationship to the next level then?"

"Yes, Myles." She sounded a bit like a schoolgirl in front of teacher to him.

"You're wondering how to let him know that short of just telling him straight out, right?"

"Yes, Myles," she agreed primly.

"Have you considered flirting?"

"Flirting?"

If he hadn't known better, he would swear she'd never heard the term before.

"Yes, pet, flirting.

* * * *

In an anteroom of Lakon's large suite, chattering and banging could be heard, punctuated by muffled swearing. Lakon, Yancey, Mya, and Myles finished their morning tea and coffee in the room's breakfast nook while they discussed their plans for the day.

Mya internally reflected on the week since that first concert she'd performed with Lakon. She'd acquired a new wardrobe just for starters. The publicity explosion had worried her and she'd put her foot down when it came to changing her hairstyle. Lakon had declared the look very sexy and had seconded her refusal, though several people from advertising seemed to think they had free reign to demand changes in every aspect of her life without so much as a *by your leave.*

The two singers had already been on a National morning show and interviewed with the largest radio show in the Boston area where they had a concert series scheduled. Mya tried hard not to seem like a country bumpkin, marveling at Lakon's smooth charm as he helped her relax and talk to the interviewer.

A photo-shoot was being prepared in the living room of his suite this morning, her first one. Therefore, the four of them were eating in a small den or what could be called an office nook. As well as the photo session, a newspaper interview was to be done at the same time. Mya didn't know if her nerves could stand it. She decided the smartest thing to do would be to follow Lakon's lead for the time being.

Claiming himself a business manager only, Yancey had gleefully turned everything over to Lakon's publicity manager in favor of driving Myles to the hospital for his treatment. Somehow, Myles and his saxophone had managed to avoid press notice and he was pleased to be "flying under the radar." This was the first time, so he'd told Mya, that he recalled being happy to need medical attention.

Mya struggled not to laugh when Lakon said, in passing, "My cousin Gene's going to handle your treatment."

"Is there a city in the United States where you *don't* have a cousin who's a doctor?" Myles asked Lakon archly as the four of them made their way into the main room.

"*No!*" Yancey and Lakon answered together. They laughed. "You know we're cousins, don't you?" Yancey asked him.

"Cor! Really?" Myles responded, a look of overdone innocent surprise on his face. It was clear that Yancey couldn't tell if the younger man meant to be serious or not.

"He's having you on, Yance," Mya told him. When he acted confused, she explained, "That means he's teasing you. You and Lakon have a tad bit of a resemblance," she told him, her eyes sweeping over Lakon's gilded good looks to stop on Yancey for an in-depth comparison.

Where Lakon's gold hair, green eyes, and prominent muscles made him look sexy and dangerous, Yancey had red brown hair, a dark cinnamon in color. Though he was well built, he wasn't as powerfully built as Lakon, though he seemed solid enough, to be sure. His eyes were a lighter green then Lakon's as well, though not pale by any means. But both men had the same chiseled features, the same arched cheekbones, and unwavering stare. She could see their family resemblance in the shape of their faces, the smooth gait, the angle of their heads when they answered or asked a question. These were two men who shared a deep connection, very much as Lakon and his brother Riker did.

Lakon turned toward her, looking down at her speculatively and causing heat to pool in the pit of her stomach.

"I'm better looking though, right baby?" he rumbled, pulling her to her feet to face him.

The looks he gave her sent her heart pounding. She placed both arms around his waist and leaned back to look at him. No question, he was the best-looking man she'd ever seen.

"Of course, my darling," she cooed. "Nobody's better looking than you."

One of the photographers setting up in the background took a picture of her playful hug.

Yancey and Myles left to go to the hospital while Lakon and Mya sat under the hot lamps and had their pictures taken.

The questions and picture-taking seemed to go on forever until Mya thought her face would crack with all the powder caked on it. She quipped that the publicity manager was making a mold of her face. She knew there'd be a mud pie on her face if she somehow got wet.

Finally, it was over and the two were alone in the room. Lakon ordered lunch sent up and banished everyone, including the annoying publicity manager. All the cameras and equipment were finally gone.

Between the heavy makeup and the sweat from the lights, Mya was so uncomfortable that Lakon sent her down the hall for a shower. She felt oily, no matter what the makeup people claimed about how breathable the gunk was.

He told her as she headed down the hall that he planned to take one as well. The pictures might look nice when they were published—they certainly hoped so, but the process was exhausting from start to finish.

When Mya came out of her shower wrapped in a bulky terrycloth robe, Lakon was only just emerging from his.

As she hurried out of the suite's main bathroom, she glanced in the direction of Lakon's room, catching him as he entered from his own en-suite. With a careless tug, Lakon discarded his damp towel exposing a half-hard erection. Mya didn't move for a moment. *What a well-sculpted, handsome man.* She stared at Lakon as he began to pull on his sweatpants. *It's now or never,* she thought.

"Wait!" she said, startling him. He pulled on his pants and froze. "Can I make you feel good, Lakon?" she asked, certain her overture was the clumsiest ever, and hoping that he'd understand her.

* * * *

What does she mean by that?

"Can I touch you there?" she asked, nodding toward his midsection, her face flaming. She took a hesitant step toward him.

"Mya," he groaned. "baby…" *She can't possibly mean what I think she means.* He was aching at the thought of her fine and delicate fingers touching his cock.

"I'd like to, Lakon," she took another step closer. He saw that her robe was tightly cinched. "Maybe if I touched you there – because I care about you – and I touch you that way – and you don't hurt me – ma - maybe it will help," she stammered. "Sort of like making friends with a nice dog after a bad dog bites you?"

Lakon couldn't help it, he laughed out loud.

He closed the distance between them. Her face was as red as the WolfPack-emblazoned sweatpants he'd pulled on in such a hurry.

"That's one hell of an analogy, baby." His eyes twinkled down at her. Putting his arms around her, he leaned down and traced her lips and chin with the tip of his tongue.

Carefully she placed her hand an inch below the elastic on his pants and pushed. She could feel his large, hard erection. It was longer than her hand. She didn't look away from his face until he groaned and closed his eyes.

"Are you sure you want to do this, baby?" he asked, sitting down on the edge of the bed and pulling her to stand between his legs.

In answer, she pushed him backwards and he pulled some pillows under his head as he reclined.

Mya reached over with both hands and tugged at the waistband on his pants. He lifted his hips so that she could work them off of him. He kicked them off and lay naked on the bed.

She scooted over to inspect him as if she'd found a box full of new toys. Reaching out with one finger, she touched his aching erection. It flexed under her finger, producing a delighted dimple. He groaned loudly, knowing he was in for a wonderful torture session at her innocent fingertips.

Extending her fingers, she petted his shaft as if it were a preening cat. It felt so good that Lakon could barely stand it. He wanted to come and didn't want to come and she was just getting started. *Oh, man!*

She wrapped her little fist around the length of him and pumped a couple of times, experimentally. He groaned again and dropped his forearm over his eyes. Then he sat up on his elbows to watch. He didn't want to miss a thing.

She seemed to be ignoring him above the waist. She was fascinated by his cock and he was fascinated by her.

Uh, oh. She had noticed the tip. He was afraid he was going to come very soon.

Smoothing her finger across the satiny hood, she touched a finger to the slit in the center. She carried that finger to her tongue and licked the clear fluid from it.

Definitely, she was going to kill him.

Rubbing her finger back and forth across the tip of his penis, she began to pump his shaft. With her other hand, she gently rubbed and caressed his balls.

She continued to pump him in a rhythmic fashion and tried to touch his tip every so often. Soon, he couldn't fight all the sensations and he felt himself beginning to come.

"Oh, Mya…oh my, baby!" he moaned as his cream jetted out onto his stomach.

She continued to massage his balls until he stopped. She reached a finger to his tip and gently touched a drop of come still there. She scooped it onto her finger and tasted it.

"Baby, you'll kill me. I just know you're going to kill me," he rumbled in a mock-groan. "It's only a matter of time."

Sliding off the bed, Mya went to the bathroom, returning with a warm washcloth, she wiped the white pool of thick cream from his tummy.

"Are you okay, now? Did I…Did I do okay?" she asked hesitantly.

He gathered her to his chest.

"Baby, you did incredible." He rested a palm on her thigh where the robe she wore parted. "I'd like to make you feel that good, too."

He began to nibble on her chin and made his way to her lower lip. His hand slowly made its way up her leg. He teased her skin behind the knee and up to her sex, but not yet touching it.

He could smell her arousal. He knew she wanted him. He was wrestling his beast with both hands now. *Down monster, down!*

"Let me touch you, Mya, let me taste you," he entreated her, his voice gravelly with want.

He lightly drew one finger over the dripping wet lips between her legs. She gasped. He covered her mouth in a drugging kiss. When she moaned his name, he deepened the kiss on a growling groan.

With one hand behind her head and the other under her bottom, he lifted her and gently laid her down in the middle of the bed. Stretching out beside her, he placed a hand on the tie to her robe.

Leaning over to lick down her neck to the vee between her breasts, he asked her, "Will you make love to me, Mya? Will you mate with me?"

"Yes," she whispered.

With a growl, he ripped open the ties to her robe and parted it. When she reached for him, he leaned over her and began to lick her breasts. He lathed them, first one and then its twin, with his hot, wet tongue until she was mewling, moaning and shifting restlessly.

His fingers slid through the dark curls between her legs and parted her dripping folds. She was so wet for him. He gently slipped a finger into her and lightly rubbed her clit with his thumb.

She cried out and bucked underneath his hand, spreading her thighs as her cream coated his fingers, her tight little breasts taut and straining.

"Taste!" he growl-groaned. "You smell so good!"

He licked and kissed his way down her body spreading her robe and rubbing his face in the tight curls covering her sex.

Using both hands, he spread her labia and tasted her with a long measured lap of his tongue, from her clit to the little opening where her sweet juices flowed.

"Mmm!" he rumbled. "So good."

The next deliberate lap began at that same little opening and ended at her clit. "More!" Lakon insisted, following action to meet his demand. He plunged his tongue inside her creaming pussy and lapped in and out, sucking at the same time and massaged her little nub while he sucked.

Her climax seemed to overtake her forcefully. Before her body stopped clenching, he slid up her body, barely hesitating above her and then pushed deep inside of her slick, clenching folds.

"Oh my *gawd*!" she screamed, clutching him to her. "Lakon! Oh!" Tears streamed down her face as she held tight to his shoulders.

"Mine!" he growled beginning to move inside of her.

After a few thrusts, he pulled out of her.

"Lakon?" she squeaked.

"Mate with me?" he sounded very guttural. What little control he had left was hanging by the thinnest thread.

"Yes? Yes! Don't stop!" she moaned.

He turned her over onto her stomach and pulled his pillows under her tummy. He tugged her to the edge of the bed. Threading his fingers through hers, he covered her with his body. His slick, hungry erection brushed against her thigh, as he licked her neck, attempting to calm himself somewhat.

Slowly, he entered her from behind. He lightly clamped his teeth on the muscle between her right shoulder and neck. His body covered hers and he began thrusting into her. He grasped a breast in one hand and rolled her nipple between his thumb and forefinger as he thrust.

"Oh, Lakon, I like that so much. Ahhhh!" she moaned to him.

"Mine, *mine*!" he growled, pounding harder and clamping his teeth more firmly into her shoulder.

She didn't seem to notice anything but the sensations flooding her tight center as her smaller body moved in concert with his.

"Say it! Mine!" he growled again, the sound rumbling from him.

"Yes, Lakon. Yours." She groaned.

"Only *mine*!" he growled again.

"Yes!" she screamed, climaxing. "Only yours. Only yours, Lakon."

The lupine roared his climax and his triumph simultaneously. Lakon collapsed on top of his mate, panting.

A minute later, he rolled to his back, taking her with him. He pulled her close, and had them both sitting up against headboard, both of them dazed and winded, and coming down from their unbelievable lovemaking.

"Mya, baby?" he queried carefully some time later as he licked at her shoulder, lathing the bite he'd made.

"Yes, Lakon?"

"You okay, baby?" her rumbled. "Was I too rough?" he leaned down and licked her shoulder again.

"I'm not sure what I am, but I'm pretty sure it's better than okay," she told him. She seemed a little dazed. "What just happened, Lakon?" She looked up at him. "I'm no expert, I know, but that seemed like…more somehow." She stared into his eyes.

"Mya, maybe what I did right now was unfair but, can you try to believe that I love you?"

She stared at him, her expression stunned. She shook her head negatively and then nodded haltingly.

"What we did, baby…" he took a deep breath. "We did what, in my family, is called "establishing a mate-bond"," he told her.

"Like with wolves?" she asked.

"Very much so. Like being married. I put my mark on you." He licked her neck and shoulder again.

She looked at him, considering.

"I should have asked you to marry me, Mya. Maybe I …"

She placed two fingers at his lips.

"I'd like to know more about your family and their way of doing things. I'd like to know you better." She relaxed against his chest. "I've lived with fear of one sort or another for a very long time," she told him. He watched her intently. "I think maybe I love you but I only know love from my brother. I would have said it was a little soon for anything so…serious. But I think I love you, too. I'm not sure, but I *think* I do…"

Lakon closed his arms around her tightly. "Want to hang out together and fuck a lot and see if we're in love?" He tilted his head and arched a brow.

She stared unblinking for a full minute. He thought he'd gone too far until she began to smile. Her smile faltered a bit.

"You promise not to hurt me, Lakon?" she asked as she looked in his eyes as if she were trying to read his soul.

"I promise," he said. It killed him that she needed this from him but he understood. "I need a promise from you, Mya," he said.

It's now or never…almost.

"Okay," she said.

"If I tell you something, you have to try to believe me. You have to remember that I will never hurt you and I will die to keep you safe. And if I ever seem or look different to you, you remember that I'm me and you're my mate? Just look in my eyes and see me, okay?"

He should tell her now – he should have told her *before* they'd made love – but he couldn't. Hopefully what he'd told her already would be enough for now.

"Okay, Lakon, I promise," she told him.

Pulling her against his body, he sighed and slid into a reclining position with her.

"Nap?" he yawned.

"Nap," she chuckled.

* * * *

The cab ride had been so long, and Mya was a nervous wreck when the taxi finally arrived at Beth Israel Deaconess Medical Center. A quick stop at the information desk to inquire after the correct floor and she was on her way.

The elevator dinged and the door opened on the Internal Medicine Wing. "I'm looking for Myles Brooks' room, please?" Mya asked the young lady behind the desk. The young, female doctor standing behind the girl sent a probing look at Mya but didn't speak. The first young woman was monitoring a bank of television screens and never looked up.

"Oh, you want the hottie in four-oh-two? Visiting hours…"

Smile somewhat strained, Mya interrupted before the woman could finish her spiel. "He's my brother, but I'll tell him you said he's a hottie."

Visiting hours weren't strictly enforced for family members, she knew. It was always like that. Myles had spent his fair share of time in the hospital over the years and she had spent a fair amount of time visiting him.

Following the nurse's instructions, she soon found herself in front of a heavy, windowless door. When Mya pushed open the door to room four-oh-two, it was dark inside. After locating a lamp, she quickly cycled through the light levels until she was satisfied with the dim glow. Moving around the side of the bed, Mya sat on the edge near her brother's waist.

"Hallo luv," she said, running her fingers through the thick hair at his forehead.

"Hi, pet," he mumbled sleepily, trying to sit up. "I'm sorry to worry you, one of the Drs. Montgomery or Livingston has found an anomaly in my blood that needs fixing or something."

"That's dead inconsiderate of you, innit?" she groused playfully as she leaned down and kissed his forehead.

"I'm definitely bad news, I am," he conceded with a tired grin.

"It's because you're a hottie. That's why they want you here. The Sisters are bored and lonely. 'S what that one at the desk said when I asked after you," Mya teased him with a chuckle, pleased when he joined her.

"How'd it go with Himself and the pictures?" he asked her.

"The pictures were a blooming pain in the arse," she winced, "but Himself made up for it all."

Realizing what she'd revealed, Mya blushed and turned her head. Myles reached up and gently tugged her face back toward his.

"You shagging the boss now, luv?" he asked her with an arched brow.

Still blushing, she said, "Not precisely this minute. More like – have shagged."

"Because you wanted to? No other reason?" He stared intently at her. Nobody knew her quite as well as her brother. Not only were they twins, but it had been just the two of them for so long.

"No other reason, sweet," she assured him with a smile.

He smiled back at her, apparently satisfied. She leaned forward into his open arms, enjoying and giving comfort for a quiet moment.

Suddenly, Mya jerked back. "Oh, no! I bet I mucked it all up!" she moaned miserably.

At his perplexed look, she explained. "We were asleep—me and Himself, I mean. I answered the phone and…"

"…When you heard I was staying in hospital, every rational thought fled your mind?" he finished for her. She groaned, nodding, and dropped her head to his chest.

"I'm such an *idiot*!" she moaned. Lakon wouldn't know where she was or why she'd left him asleep in bed. He might not forgive such a slight. Men could be *so* sensitive…

"Not even a note, pet?" Myles asked as he rubbed soothing circles on her back.

"Not the first hint of why I'm not there right now," she mumbled into his chest. "Did shag – only ever once."

She raised her head and whispered, "I knew he was safe where he was and you…" she sniffed, "what if you're not all right, Myles?" She was terrified that her brother could still die. There were never any guarantees. Myles' condition could turn ugly in one careless moment.

* * * *

Watching and listening from the bank of monitors, Lakon, who had arrived shortly after Mya, turned to Yancey.

"What does "shag" mean?" he asked.

"Good god, it means screw! You know, fuck?" groaned the young woman staring at the monitors. "Don't you even go to the movies?" she sniped, but still didn't look up.

Yancey and the young doctor who'd remained standing behind her, turned and looked at the irate girl in alarm.

"Was it a movie my brother was in?" Lakon asked uncaring, still riveted to the monitor with Myles and Mya in it. His brother, Riker Montgomery, was a successful actor with a few academy awards under his belt.

The monitor-watching girl jerked her head around and breathed, "Lakon Montgomery?"

Lakon looked at her briefly and smiled his "famous singer" smile. The girl collapsed against her chair.

"Cousin Lakon, I'm so sorry. She's – this is…" The young doctor waved a hand vaguely at the girl assigned to watch the monitors. The co-Alpha of the entire Montgomery pack had just been insulted and Lakon knew that Maisie, who was an intern now at Beth Israel Hospital, considered herself responsible.

"Don't worry about it, Maisie. Let's go down and see Myles and Mya. Yance, make sure that volume gets turned down." He arched a brow at the red-faced girl and turned toward Myles' room.

He slipped through the door quietly. Neither twin looked up.

"Imagine my surprise…" he began, Mya jerked upright and froze. In three strides, he was across the room. "I went to sleep with you in my arms and woke up alone. You won't do that again, baby?" He pulled her from her brother's arms into his own. "At least leave me a note, hmm?"

"I promise," she whispered.

Keeping an arm around Mya, Lakon reached out and shook Myles hand.

Turning to Maisie, Lakon asked, "So what's the prognosis, Dr. Maisie?"

She immediately dropped her eyes and reached for Myles' chart. "Um, I'd like to take Myles back to Duke, Cousin Lakon. I think there are a few things we can do to there that we can't do elsewhere. Dr. Jane Montgomery and Dr. Abel Livingston are involved in the testing for gene replacement therapy. They'd let me come, just because it's in line with my specialty and all…"

"Sounds good," Lakon agreed. Looking at Myles, he asked, "We're heading over to the Alltel Pavilion in a couple of days. You okay with that, Myles?"

Myles looked intently at Lakon for a few minutes. Finally, he shrugged, grinning. "I'm in, mate. It's not like I got somewhere else to be."

* * * *

When they returned to the hotel that night, Lakon guided Mya up to his suite. He ordered supper for them and they ate together, talking lightly of Myles' hospitalization and the concert series that would be ending soon.

When the meal was over and Mya had become unsure of what she should do next, Lakon pulled her into his arms.

"Mya, stay here with me," he murmured into her hair.

"Here with you, Lakon?" she repeated, a little confused.

"Stay with me in my room, in my life, in my bed, as a mate should. Stay."

She couldn't think with him holding her and kissing her as he was. That was okay. She didn't really need to think. If she weren't already in love with Lakon Montgomery, she would never have made love with him.

He must have felt her surrender to him because he swung her into his arms and carried her into the bedroom. He stripped her clothing from her tenderly, revealing more and more of her to his eager eyes and hands. He groaned his appreciation of her body as he continued his leisurely exploration. His emerald gaze traveled over her face, her mouth, hungrily sweeping her neck and shoulders.

Somehow, his own clothing floated away and she hungrily touched and stroked his bare flesh. He was hot and hard, all rippling muscles, smooth skin and soft, masculine hair darkening as it tapered from the thick blonde mat on his chest to the curly fleece framing his rod.

She felt his fingers smoothly parting her feminine lips. The touch of his fingers sent liquid heat spiraling through her, melting her insides and curling her toes. Soon she felt the smooth, round head of his shaft gliding through her body's juices as he slowly entered her.

Groaning, he pushed into her tight, moist sheath, filling her completely. He paused, letting her get used to the feeling of him.

Soon, he began to move inside her, slowly at first, then more quickly, sinking deeply inside her with each thrust. Mya held on tight, her body moving with his.

Every deep stroke built an urgent need for more, an insatiable hunger that had her hands caressing the flexing muscles of his back, squeezing his buttocks, begging incoherently for more. She found herself rising to meet his hips as he drove into her, in and out, again and again.

She heard herself crying out inarticulately as her orgasm burst over her, muscles convulsing, tightening on him and squeezing. Intense shudders controlled her body as she flew apart with her climax.

Lakon rumbled a groan into her throat as he pumped hard once more, twice and then froze, his own release whipping through him. She could feel his hot semen spurting into her and then he collapsed on top of her, replete.

* * * *

The soft *snick* of the closing door startled Myles in to full wakening. He'd dozed off shortly after Mya and Lakon left, but hospital noises never allowed him to fully rest. There were too many voices he didn't recognize, along with far too much coming and going. Add to that the fact that one never knew when someone would want more blood or who knew what else…he was never at ease in these surroundings.

"It's only me, Myles," a familiar feminine voice assured him.

More than the voice, the fact that the young lady moved toward the corner of the room before she joined him at the bed identified her as Resident Doctor Maisie Montgomery. He'd met her a few times. She was apparently something of a medical prodigy and the Montgomery Study Grant she'd been awarded allowed her to follow interesting or exceptional medical cases within the family no matter where they led. The two had been attracted to each other from the moment they'd met.

"You've turned the sound down?" he asked.

"The sound is off and the picture is dimmed. It isn't as if you're a critical case just yet…"

Myles snorted. "Your bedside manner could use a little work, Dr. Montgomery. Right now I'm left with the impression that you're rubbing your mental hands together and waiting for my systems to begin to fail."

"Oh!" Maisie dropped her face into her hands with an embarrassed squeak.

"Come now, it's not that bad. You give me something to look forward to. You *will* nurse me back to health, of course, with lots of hands on treatment?"

"You're such a tease, Myles," she accused, her head coming up to show a flushed face, barely visible in the dim light.

"'S not a tease if I mean it, sweeting," he flirted, lifting her hand and pressing his lips to her knuckle. "I'm glad you came back. Aside from generally liking you and enjoying your company, I'm a bit nervous about that bloke and my sister. You know him pretty well, then?"

"Oh, yes," Maisie gasped, sitting up straight, turning her hand so that their fingers wove together. "Lakon Montgomery is…" she stopped and appeared to consider her answer more carefully. "Well, he'd my cousin. You know that…" Myles nodded. "And he and his brother, and his father, too—they look after all of us. We're a large, close-knit family and they take responsibility for all of us. He's very important to us. Him and his brother, Riker," she added quickly. "Both of them are really, *very* important to us."

Myles searched eyes for countless seconds. There was something fervent about her declarations, as if she hoped to make him believe by sheer force of will. It made him a bit uneasy, as if her eyes were actually glowing.

"Well, I'll keep that in mind, then, shall I?" he hedged. "I've worked with him for around two years. He's been pretty decent and Yancey's been a right mate to me these last few weeks. Now, what about you, Miss Montgomery?" he asked, looking pointedly at their linked hands. "I think we should get to know each other better, don't you? In the interests of possible family relations, of course…"

Maisie blushed prettily and allowed Myles to take her other hand. "Well, since I'm really not your doctor, more of an observer and consultant…and anyway, it does look like your sister might ma-marry Lakon…" Myles wondered what she'd meant by that but nodded in agreement. He knew his sister felt strongly about Lakon Montgomery. Marriage was a real possibility between Lakon and Mya. "We *should* get to know each other better…"

"And then there's the part where I'm attracted to you and you're attracted to me, hmm?" he murmured as his hand moved up her arm to cup the back of her head and apply gentle pressure.

Maisie leaned in, allowing it. "That, too," she breathed as his lips brushed hers lightly.

"Mmm," Myles agreed, letting his lips skim back and forth. They didn't really know each other yet, but this was a hell of an ice breaker. When she pulled back, he let her, smiling slightly as she glanced around furtively.

"Maybe I should go?" she stuttered. "I can come back tomorrow…" If her face got any redder, Myles feared she'd burst into flames.

"Join me for brekkie?" he invited, stroking her cheek with one finger.

"I'd like that," she agreed, slightly breathless.

"See you then."

He closed his eyes as she righted the camera and sound feed, allowing his breathing to even out. By the time he heard the door open and close behind her, he was almost asleep. He couldn't remember the last time he'd even considered dating someone. It felt good, nice. The peaceful idea of it all stayed with him until he drifted off.

* * * *

"Hey! Wake up!"

Myles shot straight up in bed, nearly hanging himself on the IV tubing that had pulled taut across his throat when he'd fallen asleep with his hand tucked under his cheek. "What?" he croaked looking around in alarm until his eyes landed on the grinning man in the doorway. "Think I can get money for this tape?" Yancey asked, raising one hand to show a small camcorder which he trained on Myles. "Smile, pretty boy," he crooned.

"What are you on about, ya berk?" Myles snapped, still more than a little disoriented. "What's that?"

Yancey moved into the room, hooking the bedside chair with one foot and sinking into it when he judged it close enough. "See?" He held up a silver and black device that had an obvious lens on one end, though Myles couldn't identify any other part of it. "It's a camcorder, so you're not the only one on camera anymore!" he chortled proudly. "I figure you get bored here, nothing to do but watch TV and flirt with the nurses."

Myles grinned, and then chuckled. "You know, mate, most people bring a magazine or a box of sweets."

Yancey shrugged and leaned forward, tilting Myles' mattress until he sat up completely. "I'm not most people. I like gadgets." He trained a beady eye on Myles. "You've done sound and lights for this dog and pony show for two years now. Don't try and tell me you don't like electronics."

Reaching for the camcorder, Myles shook his head in denial. "No, mate, I'm not saying that at all. I love buttons and bells. The shinier, the better. What's this one do?" he asked, touching an oblong green button on the side.

"No! Don't touch that one!" Yancey yelped, reaching to grab the device away from Myles.

"What? Why not?"

"I wanted to be first!" Yancey whined.

"Hey! It's my new toy and I'm sick in the bed. You've got to let me play with it first."

"All right, but only if I get to try that one," Yancey countered, pointing to a small grey button.

After a brief consideration, Myles shrugged. "Suits me. Now then, lean back so I can get your whole face in the shot." He held the wide button clearly labeled record and then pressed the green button. "Oh, wicked. It changes the colors so you look …sepia, I guess it's called."

"Nice. My turn." Yancey stood and took the camcorder, stepping back to record. After several seconds, he pushed the small grey button. "Oh." He looked a Myles and back down at the small display screen. "It's blank. It erased the whole thing."

"Don't suppose that new toy came with instructions, did it?" Myles asked.

Yancey looked at him in disbelief. "Where's the fun in that?" Rolling his eyes Myles flopped back on the bed. "Fine," Yancey huffed, dropping a fat little book on the mattress next to Myles' elbow. "If this doesn't keep you busy, nothing will." He handed Myles the camera. "Be right back. I need to see what's keeping room service."

Myles watched his new friend leave the room. This was far and away the bet hospital stay he'd ever had. He lifted the device to his face and pressed the record button. Thanks to Yancey, he'd have a video to commemorate the event, too. Things could be worse.

Chapter 7

A week had passed since the turbulent night that Myles had been admitted to the hospital. Lakon, Mya and their working entourage finally arrived at the Alltel Pavilion in Raleigh, North Carolina. Myles had been transferred to Duke University Medical Center days ago. She'd finally visited him the night before. It seemed like a long trip for Mya, without Myles there beside her, but she'd ridden with Lakon in his bus, and it had been quite the experience.

Now, she was in the center of the huge outdoor arena, heading down toward the stage when she saw Lakon there already, but he wasn't alone. She stopped and watched as he dropped to his knees in front of a beautiful blonde.

She felt no jealousy toward the other woman. She was confident that Lakon loved only her. He hadn't said it again since the first time they'd made love but she believed he felt it. They'd automatically shared a room when they arrived in North Carolina and it felt right. Everything about their relationship felt right.

It wasn't as if they got along every second. Of course they argued a bit. She wasn't a pushover and needless to say, Lakon liked having his own way, whether she agreed or not. They usually worked things out, though she was well aware that their relationship was still in its "honeymoon" stage. She intended to be in this for the long haul, and so, it seemed, did Lakon.

Mya looked forward to the four-month break they'd soon have. He'd spoken little about what he hoped to do during the break but mentioned introducing her to his family. The last two years when it had been just herself and Myles, they'd taken part-time jobs in the foothills of North Carolina. She knew the area well.

On the stage below her, Lakon wrapped both arms around the woman's hips and pressed his ear to her abdomen as if he were listening to something. Unmoving, still halfway up the auditorium, Mya stood staring, her mind whirring, knowing there was something in her memory about this woman. She'd never met her but she should know who she was.

Suddenly, her attention was torn from the stage by the feeling of a hard body pressed against her own from behind, touching her from head to heels. One strong arm came around her middle and the other hand plunged into her hair, tugging gently until she allowed her head to angle, exposing her neck and right shoulder. Fear shot through her and her mind froze for long moments.

"Mmm, you are very sweet and tasty, lovely Mya," a deep, masculine voice rumbled into her throat at her clavicle. When she felt him lick her there, she gasped. "You smell beautiful," the big man purred. "My brother is a very lucky man." He began to massage her scalp.

"Mr. Montgomery, please…" It had to be the famous actor, Riker Montgomery – Lakon only had the one brother, she remembered, though how her mind was even functioning through her panic, she didn't know. She pulled against his arm and the hand in her hair tightened. She tried to struggle but he held her immobile. "Let me go, Mr. Montgomery, please?" she forced weakly through her dry throat.

"Call me Riker, honey," he murmured, dragging his lips back and forth over her neck and shoulder in an intimate caress. "We're a very close-knit family. Just call me Riker."

She continued to struggle ineffectually, until the big man growled low in his throat. She froze instantly, standing very still, afraid to move. Somehow, she knew this wasn't a come-on. She felt like a juicy bone.

"Take your hands – and your mouth – off of my mate," rumbled Lakon menacingly.

"But brother, I'm just having a little conversation with my beautiful and tasty new sister. There's nothing but love here," he crooned into her throat, his tongue darting out to lick her warm skin.

Before she knew what was happening, the brothers were actually snarling at each other and she was sandwiched in between them. Shaking, she stood immobile, certain that one wrong move would have these big, muscular men growling, biting and ripping at one another – with her a bloody casualty in between.

Riker rubbed his cheek against Mya's while he continued to caress her scalp. Lakon's flashing green eyes glared in fury at the man behind her. He didn't even seem to realize that she was there.

"Help?" she all but prayed. She was unable to emit more than a thin, frightened squeak.

"Stop that you two!" A very angry, very beautiful blonde woman had made her way up to them. It was the same woman that Lakon had been embracing minutes earlier. "Just because your father isn't here doesn't mean you can act like wild dogs! Riker, you let go of your brother's mate right now before I take her and go to the islands for a girls' weekend!"

The woman sounded credibly threatening and reached between the brothers, tugging Mya free. She could feel herself shaking. The other woman wrapped an arm around her and marched her down a few more steps before stopping.

Leaving Mya standing, the woman whirled to face the still-snarling men, stomping back up the few steps. "Making a pregnant woman run uphill like that," she growled. Riker and Lakon began to look a little shame-faced. The woman got right up in each man's face as she finished yelling at one and then the other. "If we want male companionship at all, we'll find someone who'll treat us like beautiful women, not a bowl of moist kibble."

She marched back down the stairs and slipped an arm around Mya's waist mumbling, "Just keep walking. You can't let 'em smell your fear. It just makes 'em feel tough." A few seconds later, the blonde whispered, "It helps if you get mad, it kind of wipes out the fear smell."

* * * *

The other woman led Mya right out the door of the building. She waved and a long black car smoothly pulled up next to her, a driver hopping out and opening the door.

"I'm Bethany Black Montgomery, Riker's wife," the blonde woman told Mya as the two women seated themselves in the car..

"I was sure I knew your face from somewhere. I was just trying to place how I recognized you when… when your husband… um…" Mya didn't want to make the other woman mad. She had no woman friends and this one seemed handy to have around.

"I'm really sorry about Riker. Somehow I thought he was more mature than that. Lakon's been teasing him since we first met. He's never teased his brother as bad as what Riker did with you, though. I really can't believe he'd take a chance like that. I guess the words "mature" and "man" don't belong in the same sentence." She was giggling now. Mya couldn't help herself and began to giggle, too.

"So you don't think they'll actually fight?" Mya asked when they'd settled down. She was still pretty worried about how both bestial the men had been acting. "They're both pretty growly."

"Yeah but it's just a lot of noise. They'll just growl and brood. What has Lakon told you about himself and his family?" Bethany asked her.

"Um, not too much," Mya began. "He says that being growly is a family trait and that they're very primal."

After they'd been riding for a few minutes, the new friends spotted a cafe and the driver turned in to it, per Bethany's instruction.. They were seated right away, and served quickly enough.

Returning to their interrupted conversation, Bethany repeated, "He said they're primal?" and expelled a heavy breath. "That's an understatement," she sighed. "Nothing else?"

"Well, he said we'd established a mate-bond, like...wolves I guess..." Mya wrinkled her brow. "Like being married, but not married, he said."

"The man's an idiot, pure and simple," Bethany stated, aggravation warring with the open affection on her face. Mya looked at her, alarmed. "I'm sorry. I guess my temper's pretty short, these days. I'm about to have another baby and that makes *me* growly, sometimes." She laughed to herself. "I guess that's why we left our twin boys with Riker's mother this time!"

"How did you meet Riker and Lakon?" Mya asked the lovely blonde.

Bethany laughed. "That's a story for a pitcher of margaritas! I met Riker by accident and got separated from him. It really *is* a long story. The first time I met Lakon, I was walking down the highway in the freezing cold and he gave me a lift. It was a well-choreographed coincidence, to be sure."

"Wow! I'm sure you were glad of the ride, weren't you?" Mya asked, fascinated.

"Not really. Not then. See, I didn't know if I could trust Riker and Lakon right then. In fact, a little later he pulled the car over and I jumped out. He tackled me and I sprayed ammonia in his eyes." She shook her head, remembering. "I can't believe he ever spoke to me again after that. Of course, a two-hundred-something pound man tackling you in gravel leaves quite an impression, too!"

"One of these days, I'd really like to hear the whole story, Bethany. That is, if..." Mya began.

"Don't worry, Mya, you and I will have that girls' weekend and get roasted and toasted. I'll tell you every detail!" Bethany promised with an engaging grin.

After that, the two women talked for a while about how that evening's concert would be the last in the current series. Bethany spoke of introducing Mya to the rest of the family if she chose to join them in the upcoming days.

Mya, in turn, explained that her brother, Myles, was in the hospital at Duke University Medical Center and that she planned to stay close by until his treatment ended.

When they finished their coffee, Bethany pulled out a card and scribbled a number onto it. "I like you, Mya. I really like you. One day soon, you may need someone to talk to. Just call me, okay?"

"Okay," Mya agreed. The conversation ended there, with the two women climbing back into the car that had awaited them, and the driver automatically turning back toward the amphitheater.

Chapter 8

The concert went well but Mya noticed that Lakon had been acting oddly all day. When she had returned with Bethany, Lakon steered her roughly away from Bethany and Riker and they'd begun to rehearse as they meant to do before their interruptions.

Lakon had been equally short tempered at lunch when Riker and Yancey brought another man to join them. Bethany seemed happy to see the man and he'd been polite to Mya.

"Tav, Tavist Darke, is a very dear friend of our family," Bethany explained to her. "He's like a brother to all three of us, four, I mean," she corrected quickly, including Yancey. "We just call him Tav," she ended on a faltering note. Mya certainly understood. With the way the four men were staring, unblinking, it was absolutely unnerving.

"Nice to meet you, Tav," Mya said politely, shaking the dark-haired man's hand. Lakon had given her a hard look and while she couldn't understand the anger in his gaze, she gave a mental shrug and thought no more about it.

During that night's concert, Lakon pulled her roughly away from one of the band members when she'd strolled too close to him during their duet. He'd played it off as smitten, Neanderthal behavior, but it made Mya uncomfortable. Later, as she was explaining to a new roadie how best to store some of the equipment, Lakon had demanded that she leave with him immediately.

Now, in the room they shared, Mya turned to Lakon who was pacing. He'd begun a controlled circuit of the room as soon as the door had closed, and the air was heavy with tension.

"Lakon, you seem awfully tense. What's wrong?" she asked him.

"Now why would anything be wrong, baby?" he growled. "I love watching my mate check out other men all day. Did you enjoy snuggling up to my brother this morning?"

"Lakon, what on earth?" She was incredulous. "Where is this coming from? Bethany said you two do that to be mean to each other. I certainly didn't want him to…"

"Oh, you didn't want a famous actor to rub all over you and suck on your neck? You sure, baby?" He advanced on her as she backed toward their bedroom. "I've been in the movies. I'm not good enough now?"

"You're acting ridiculous Lakon Montgomery! If I were interested in another man do you think I'd try to pick him up right in front of you? I'm not stupid!" she snapped angrily, stomping her foot in agitation.

"No, baby, no, you're not stupid, not at all. Maybe you're just feeling neglected," he offered, his voice oddly low and suggestive. "I'm not giving you the attention you so badly need, am I? Maybe you want me to make love… differently? Is that it?"

He continued to crowd her, his hands skimming over her hungrily. He was making her uncomfortable – he wasn't acting like the man that she loved.

"Lakon, stop, this isn't…" He reached forward and ripped her dress in half. She tripped, backing away. "Don't! Lakon. Stop!"

She turned to run into the other room. Grabbing her from behind, he ripped the thin designer dress she wore. His hands weren't bruising on her skin, but he was definitely intent upon one goal. She squirmed and wriggled as he tugged the torn material from around her as if it were paper. His arm around her waist held her still against him while his other hand brushed her thin silk and elastic away with ease.

"Which is it, baby?" He growled from behind her, "Don't or don't stop? You want something I'm not giving you, don't you?" His moth was at her ear, hot breath fanning her cheek.

"Lakon, I love you, I like how we make love!" Mya felt the thrill of excitement that was always present when Lakon touched her intimately, but this time, it was tempered by fear. Whatever he wanted, love, sex, it didn't matter, he was angry and his anger frightened her.

"Don't you like this, Mya baby?"

She heard his zipper being lowered and felt his hard erection against her naked rear-end. "I don't know what I did but I only love you!"

"I love you, Mya, you're *mine*!" he growled.

With a low guttural growl that sounded as if it came from deep inside, Lakon's jaw clamped onto her shoulder muscle and Mya vaguely thought she could hear the sound of his teeth meeting. Still growling, he lifted her onto his jutting cock. Mya tensed, she wasn't ready, and couldn't help crying out as she felt him push his way into her, stretching her wide, wider than she thought possible.

She had been dry at first and it hurt, tearing her tender opening. Lowering her to the floor, he covered her body with his. He began pumping into her, pinning her in place with his body and his hands. His teeth held her immobile, still embedded in her shoulder.

She bucked, trying to struggle against him, trying not to let fear take over. The thrashing, bucking movement slammed her rounded cheeks against his lower belly and he stilled. She realized he'd stopped, and she froze, afraid to move.

Lakon braced himself on one arm and wrapped his other around her waist. He gripped her tightly as he shook his head, as if he couldn't help himself, and then gently disengaged his jaw. He silently licked the bite, soothing her, calming her.

He began to move inside her once again, slowly easing in and out. He was still angry; she could feel his tension, the tautness of his muscles, the tight control. It was obvious that he was keeping himself on a firm leash, and she dare not move in case it snapped. Her fear receded just enough for her body to recognize Lakon as her mate, and unbelievably, arousal started to curl through her. Before she could adjust any further he pumped one final time, his rod pulsing in her core, and he growled his climax into her shoulder and collapsed on top of her.

Mya didn't move. She barely breathed. She could see Lakon's green eyes glowing in the moonlit room. Again, his jaw clamped around the muscle between her neck and shoulder and he gave it a rough shake, letting it go and licking it.

He lifted himself off of her and stood. He zipped his pants and left the room. A minute later, she heard the door open and close as he left their suite. Still, Mya waited. He'd gone from affectionate to enraged in seconds and she had no real idea why. She was grateful that he'd restrained himself, somewhat – that he'd recognized what he was doing and somehow managed to control himself a little. Still, it was as if he'd been another man entirely – a man she wasn't sure she could live with. He'd been jealous and out of control, and very frightening because of it.

When she was sure he wouldn't be back, Mya quickly showered and dressed in old jeans and one of Lakon's old shirts. The bite at the curve of her neck hurt, it was in need of attention. She took the time to pour some twenty-five year old scotch onto the wound and then rinsed it with water, leaving a folded towelette pressed firmly atop it.

Quickly, she packed a small backpack with two spare long sleeved shirts, extra panties, a pair of his sweat pants and a second pair of her jeans. She rolled a hotel blanket up and secured it to her bag. She needed to make haste before he returned.

Finally, she found a first aid kit in the bathroom and bandaged her wound as best she could. She knew there would be muscle and tendon damage. Everything that she didn't use from the first-aid kit went into her backpack. Her wound would need more attention over the next few days or it could become seriously infected.

Mya stuffed some of Lakon's socks into her backpack, too, and grabbed a well-lined leather jacket that was his. It was bulkier than the jackets she owned and she could wear more layers under it. She tied one of his sweatshirts around her waist. It was chilly out these days and would only get cooler as the days went on. She had no idea when she would return, so it only made sense to be prepared. Not only that, but dressing down as she was would keep her from being spotted by her newly-acquired fans. That would be *terribly* inconvenient.

Looking around the room, she stuffed portable snacks into her bag and into her coat pockets. Deciding that she'd taken as long as she dared, Mya looked for and found the hotel stationary.

She decided to keep her note to Lakon short, but honest, so she wrote:

Lakon,
You hurt me. I don't know why. I need to go think about things.
I'll always love you.
Mya

She took a Band Aid and taped the note to the head of the bed. After straightening the room a little and disposing of her torn dress, she left the room.

* * * *

When Lakon arrived back at the suite hours later, he was filled with remorse. He realized that his behavior toward Mya had been inexcusable. Even that word didn't articulate his out of control behavior. He decided to punish himself by sleeping on the couch and letting Mya get some rest. It was clear she'd already gone to bed. He'd beg forgiveness in the morning and be prepared to so whatever it took to make it up to her.

The run he'd had with his brothers and members of his pack had cleared his head. He and Riker had gone at each other for several moments, jaws flashing and locking together in painful accusation.

Lakon had been too affectionate to Bethany, his hands on her stomach as he'd listened to the coming pup within. But Riker had taken uncalled for liberties with Lakon's mate. The mating was too new and Riker too strong for such actions to be interpreted as anything be threats to his mate-bond. They'd both been out of line and needed to be more careful—that had been the understanding they'd come away with by the end of the night.

Awakening late the next morning on the couch, Lakon struggled to remember why he was there instead of the bed. He felt a little out of it still, his hormones had been surging, like a drug in his veins. Finally, it hit him. Mya. He'd been rough with her the night before.

He'd been more than rough – he'd taken her in anger – nearly raping her. Now that he thought about things, he realized that his behavior had been irrational even before that. He'd let Riker's stunt that morning push him over the edge and he'd taken it out on Mya.

Mya… His stomach fell to his knees. Her scent was fainter this morning. He extended his senses, considering what they told him of his surroundings. Faint scent and no noises. The suite was too quiet. No matter how late she stayed up, his mate was usually awake by this time of morning.

With his lupine hearing, he should be able to hear her roll over in bed, even with the door closed. At least he'd hear the even breathing of her sleeping or the furtive noises of her trying to be quiet.

It was as silent as a tomb in his suite. A tomb—the macabre comparison made him shudder. The suite was empty and he knew it. Once again, as he had so many times before, he felt a fleeting empathy for his brother and the pain he'd suffered while searching for Bethany. No quiet had ever seemed as quiet as this room without Mya in it. Dread swamping him like an icy cloak, Lakon forced himself to get up and go to the bedroom he'd shared with her. Standing in the doorway, he looked around. As it was meant to, her note taped with buff colored adhesive strip caught his eye immediately.

She'd told him last night that she loved him. Twice she'd told him. The scene played a never-ending loop in his brain. Now, he held the same message in writing. She loved him. She loved him, but she was gone. Lakon dropped to his knees and howled, the sound no doubt echoing through the halls of the over-priced hotel.

Chapter 9

When Lakon stormed into his hospital room, Myles was waiting for him. Before his boss could open his mouth, Myles began to speak.

"Take the video, take the camera. Watch the tape." He indicated them with a jerky sweep of his hand. When Lakon would have spoken, Myles cut him off, his voice tight with controlled anger. "Don't come back here today. Somebody will let you know if I can stand to look at you tomorrow." He resolutely closed his eyes and rolled to his side, turning his back on him.

As he lay back in his bed, eyes closed so he wouldn't have to look at the window across from him, Myles considered all that had happened. Mya was hurt. She had gone and it was all that man's fault. He knew that Mya would be back, so it wasn't like he wouldn't see her again. But she had felt the need to get away.

It was all Lakon Montgomery's fault. The werewolf factor—that wasn't really all that big a shocker. All those nights lying atop the parked busses…he'd seen the silhouettes of the coyotes and wolves, most likely *all* wolves in light of tonight's revelations. Regardless, taken proportionately, there were more wolves to be seen when those busses were parked than nature in general could excuse. But people saw what they wanted to see, didn't they?

Myles was no stranger to that concept. When he and his sister lived at home with their parents, the abuse hadn't really been all that well hidden. It had been inconvenient, but not invisible. Therefore, it was ignored—the elephant in the room that strangers cheerfully worked around, clucking sadly at Mya's apparent clumsiness, shaking their heads in concern at Myles pale complexion and too thin stature.

He didn't know what he'd do about the rest of these Montgomerys. It was safe to say his feelings were mixed. Maisie Montgomery took pretty good care of him, and she was pretty. He was more than a little attracted to her.

"Myles?" Maisie stood in the doorway to his hospital room. "Are you okay? You've seemed…upset all day."

He studied her closely for several beats. *Was* he okay? "No, Maisie, I really don't think I am."

"You know you can talk to me, Myles," she assured him, moving into the room and closing the door behind her. "I just saw Mr.

66

Montgomery leave, is that what you're upset about? Did something happen between you two?"

He pushed himself upright in the bed, reaching for the control mechanism to adjust the mattress more comfortably. "Something happened between him and my sister, and yes, me, too." He thought it over briefly. "You like me, don't you, Maisie? Want to go out when I get out of here, yes?"

Now perched facing him on the bed, she leaned in slightly. "I do, Myles, of course I do," she assured him earnestly. "I thought we'd both been sort of clear on that. I kind of thought we were already becoming a couple…"

"So did I, Maisie. But species disclosure is important to us human sorts. Were you planning to tell me that you were a werewolf? Or didn't you think I would want to know?"

Maisie looked like the proverbial "deer in headlights" or, Myles supposed, perhaps *wolf* in headlights was more appropriate under the circumstances.

"I-I," Maisie stumbled, completely blindsided. "I'm, *we're* not supposed to say anything unless it's serious." Myles arched a brow. *Now that's a telling statement if ever I've heard one. Maybe I should've gone with Mya after all.* "I mean, well, we don't *always* recognize...that is…"

Heaving a great sigh, Myles took pity on the stuttering young woman. While somewhere in the back of his mind, or perhaps nearer the front than he'd thought, he'd considered Maisie a serious relationship. It was true that they hadn't had an opportunity to do much in the way of dating, but they'd kissed, spent hours on end together and talked a great deal about personal interests and feelings. He cared about her and had begun to think of life after the hospital. Perhaps he was more naive than his sister.

"Never mind, Maisie," he interrupted. He was tired and it sounded in his voice. Tired inside and out. "Just forget it. Why don't you go on. We can talk later, hmm?"

"Myles? I…it wasn't…"

"Just go for now, Maisie. We'll talk later." He wanted nothing more at this moment than to be alone. Perhaps he should have been more considerate of the young woman's discomfort, but he couldn't find it in himself to care right now. Maybe later. Myles rolled to his side, facing away from Maisie and the door. "Go on, Maisie. Close the door, will you?"

He had a lot to sort out in his head right now, and didn't need to worry over her, too. It was bad enough that he'd signed on the dotted line and now he and his sister were indefinitely entangled with Lakon Montgomery and his family.

Truthfully, before the events of last night, Myles had liked Lakon. Werewolf or not, he would still like Lakon, except that the bastard hurt his little sister. If the rest of the clan thought that was A-okay, then there was a problem.

Well. There was a problem anyway. The size of said problem would be directly proportionate to what the next Montgomery he met had to say for himself. He didn't think it would be Lakon. That fur-bearing bastard had better get himself off to find Mya. The angriest part of Myles still wanted to hurt the man, but he'd respect his sister's wishes for awhile longer.

* * * *

Lakon, Riker, Yancey, Tavist and Bethany sat down in Lakon's hotel suite. Lakon had inserted the tape into the complimentary VCR and turned it on, sitting back to see what happened next. He really didn't care anymore who saw what was on the recording, as long as he could see it also.

As the video began to play, they were treated to rustling and then a view of the night sky through the hospital window. There was a full moon showing through the glass which meant that tape had been made last night.

"I'm just going to stand over here for now, luv," Mya's voice said. "Let's make a midnight movie." Mya was the one with the video camera, apparently.

"I know we're night owls, Pet, but I thought you had a warm body at home to keep you indoors on nights like this?" Myles asked. His voice sounded worried.

Mya could be heard swallowing before she answered. "Himself is out enjoying the night air, just now." Lakon felt the knot of foreboding in his chest grow tighter.

"Is that what's wrong, sweet? He's left you in while he chases other skirts? You think that's…"

"Um, no, Myles, that's not it. We had a bit of a spat, if you will. He's been in a twist all day and fair exploded a while ago."

The camera seemed to shake a little and then stilled. Lakon knew the effort it cost her to still her shaking hand.

"Did he hurt you, Mya, did he?" Myles' voice took on a hard edge.

The camera panned left across the view of terrain through the window and then back to the right, stopping to focus on a group of people in a nearby field, on the backside of the hospital wing.

Lakon knew what was coming next, he recognized the scenery and view from the window of Myles' hospital room. Murmuring could be heard from Riker, Yancey and Tav, obviously, they were figuring things out as well. Bethany and Lakon just stared at the screen.

"Earlier, I was going to tell you that he was out chasing his tail and howling at the moon," Mya croaked on the television. "Seems he really is."

The picture had zoomed in to show one person on the edge of the crowd transform into a wolf.

"What're you on about?" Myles' voice sounded closer now.

Another person on the screen changed into a wolf.

"My? Come hold the camera." It changed hands with barely a ripple. The camera focused on Lakon as he changed. "So, if I said that I saw the man I love change into a really big dog?"

"If you were alone, luv, I'd say you were barmy." Myles' normally smooth, rich voice had a definite wobble now. He cleared his throat and leaned, causing the camera to jostle.

"Since I'm not?"

"Handsome brute, inn'ee?" Myles observed.

"Dead sexy, he is, even in fur," she agreed. "There goes his brother. I saw Bethany at the hotel when I left so…" Mya let that sentence hang.

"Blimey! That's Maisie."

"Must be what they meant by their family being primal, huh?" Mya mumbled.

"Yeah, guess so… There's Yancey." The man in question stirred, eyes focused on the television, but seeming a tad embarrassed.

"That explains a lot, really," Mya said. "No one looks Lakon or Riker in the eyes. They must be Alpha and Beta or something."

Riker arched a brow and looked over at his brother who shrugged.

"Yeah? How's it feel being hooked up with the big bad wolf, luvvie?" Myles let out a nervous laugh.

On the screen, the two largest wolves, one brown and one blonde, turned toward the wood line and bounded out of view.

"I'm not saying this doesn't bother me, darling, oh god it does, but I was leaving anyway. I came to see if you want to stay or go."

At hearing Mya say those words, Lakon leaned back in his chair and expelled a breath, moisture gathering in his eyes. He didn't want to take his eyes of the television screen, but it hurt, how it hurt to hear her say that. And it was his fault.

"Mya?" Her brother sounded worried again.

"I might be able to deal with my husband having a secret life as a wolf, even though he didn't trust me enough to tell me about it. And he *is* my husband, I guess, according to his own beliefs, and in my own heart. It's just that there are too many things he doesn't trust me about, Myles. I need to go think. I can't stay right now."

Her shadow could be seen leaning down to switch on a dim light since Myles was still holding the camera. Those watching the tape could see she'd been crying. The men in the room looked at Lakon for a second and then back at the screen.

Mya turned her back to her brother and said, "He turned into a snapping, snarling beast before he changed into a wolf, Myles. He thinks I want to bonk somebody else."

The flannel shirt she wore, one of Lakon's, slid off of her shoulders and exposed her bare upper back. At the curve where the right shoulder met her neck was a large blood-covered gauze bandage. Myles' hand could be seen gingerly tugging at it, exposing a large and seeping, bite-shaped wound with four punctures – two on either side of the shoulder. The injury was clearly visible from Myles' higher vantage.

"Bloody fucking arse-wipe, bung hole, bleeding son of a bitch, mother humping, bum sucking son of a whore," Myles gritted in a low voice. Yancey's eyes went wide in shock at the filthy diatribe, as did Bethany's.

"You kiss your mother with that mouth?" Mya whispered, a choking laugh tangled with a sob punctuating the words.

"No, only ever my lovely little sister. I'm getting someone in here to fix that, pet." His voice was shaking with anger.

"Don't call anyone, My, don't!" she said in a frightened voice. "*You* have to do it. We don't know who's who right now and if he's Alpha or Beta …"

On the screen the camera was lowered to the windowsill and taped the full moon reflecting off the glass while the twins spoke.

"Shhh, little sister, shhh. Don't worry," he soothed her. "I'll take care of it. It needs to be tighter." They could hear the tearing sounds of a new bandage being put in place. It was not uncommon for nurses and aides to leave simple supplies in the hospital rooms of patients in frequent need of bandaging or dressing changes. "Can you stand that?" Myles asked gently.

"S'okay." She spoke through gritted teeth, pain evident in her voice.

"Can you give me one good reason not to kill that bastard, or die trying?" Myles spoke again after a minute. The whispering sound of his slipper-footed steps brushing on carpet grew louder as he walked toward the video recorder. The picture shook as he lifted the device and turned.

"I have three." Myles trained the camera on Mya to show her talking. She was pale and shaking a little. "First, dogs have thicker skin and stronger neck muscles than people do." She seemed to know what she was talking about.

"So you're saying that the son of a bitch, no pun, forgot you weren't one of his *kind* and bit you too hard? Completely by accident, of course." Lakon squirmed in his seat hearing Myles's disgust.

"Yeah, I guess. And second, you know he doesn't know his own strength. We talked about that when you got hurt."

"I don't care how strong a man is, Mya, he should remember his strength around his woman, no excuses. Bastard!" Myles spat. "What's the third reason?"

"I love him, Myles. It doesn't matter if he's a rat, a rabbit, or a hyena – I love him. I'm just going to love him from a distance now. You coming?" Myles set the camera down. The screen showed him moving to stretch out on the bed and her curling up beside him.

"No, luv, I think I'll stay. I may have feelings for Maisie and, fool that I am, I want to see where things go, even if she is a..."

"Lupine," Mya finished for him.

"Lupine." He repeated. "Maybe it won't work out. I'm not sure which of us is the lion or the lamb in this relationship, if there is one. Where're you heading? North or South?"

"North, I guess. Maybe northeast. The mountains are big enough to hide in while I sort things out."

"He might come looking for you, pet." Mya could be heard sniffling a little. A tear trickled down her face, followed quickly by several more. She angrily rubbed them away with the heel of her hand.

"Can't imagine why...He apparently thinks I want to have a hump with his brother, his best friend, the guy at lunch, the drummer, and the roadies." She'd managed to get control her spate of tears.

"Anybody that jealous will probably wonder where his favorite toy rolled off to, pet," Myles pointed out as he rhythmically combed his hand through her hair.

"Well, I guess you won't know where I am until I tell you, will you?" She sounded a little angry again as Myles reached for the bed's controls and pushed a button, causing the mattress to fold upright and bringing the couple into a sitting position. "Therefore, you can't rat me out, can you?"

"Just drop an ad in the big local so I'll know you're set, okay? There's *"The Herald Sun"* and *"The Raleigh News and Observer"*."

"I'm set, Myles. I know a vet that will help me with this bite. Won't ask too many questions."

She kissed her brother and hugged him tightly. From his place on the bed, Myles had hefted the camera again and was following her movements.

Lakon watched as she lifted a bag with her left hand and walked from the room. All went quiet on the screen and after a short while, Myles reached over and turned the camcorder off.

* * * *

Lakon stared at the dark screen for long minutes, not really even sure how to react. He'd hurt her. More than that, he'd injured her, and now Mya had left him.

"Well?" Riker demanded, stepping in front of him, blocking his view of the television. He hadn't even heard his brother stand up.

"Well what?" Lakon asked, still feeling dazed. He looked up at his brother. "What do I do, Rike? What...what should I do? I didn't...I don't..."

A rustling and shifting sounded the exodus of the rest of the group, though a quick glance at the door showed Yancey leaning against it.

"You hurt your mate, Lake. Why? You bit her pretty hard it looks like." Riker's tone was gentle, almost understanding, but his eyes were hard. Lakon couldn't imagine Riker ever doing such a thing to Bethany. What was wrong with him?

"I don't know why...I mean, it was like a fire in my blood. Everyone was looking at her, touching her, and you...man, I know you'd never...but when you put your mouth on her it...I couldn't handle it, Rike. I'm not fit. I should be put down."

At that, Yancey stormed over to him and bodily lifted him from his chair, throwing him to the floor. The move took Lakon completely by surprise and before he could put up even the most token struggle, Yancey jerked him back just far enough to slam him back down to the floor, causing stars to flash in front of his eyes briefly.

"Shut the fuck up, you worthless cur," he growled, his angry breath fanning Lakon's face. "You hurt her because you can't control your fucking dog impulses. You get off your mangy ass and go find her and then you crawl on your knees and beg, that's what you do!"

Lakon had no doubt that Yancey would have slammed him into the floor again if not for Riker's intervention. "Yancey, come on..." Riker lifted Yancey off of Lakon and dangled him in the air by one hand, looking at the door and the couch before making up his mind. He dropped Yancey on the couch and held a hand up, palm out. "Stay!" he barked, turning back toward Lakon and extending his hand.

Lakon took it and struggled to his feet, feeling the back of his head carefully. "I fucked up, I know that," he mumbled, the sting of tears prickling his eyes.

"That's a start, brother," Riker murmured, steering him to a chair. "I think one of us will need to go back and talk to her brother, Lake. I don't think it should be you."

Lakon glanced over at Yancey. "I'm not so sure I want to help you find her, cousin," Yancey snarled. "I think you should work for it."

"Yance..."

"You told her you wouldn't hurt her. You promised her brother you wouldn't hurt her. If you can't control yourself..." Yancey shot to his feet and paced to the window, his back to the two brothers. "I wonder what Uncle Mik's going to say?"

Lakon blanched, feeling lightheaded. He felt bad enough that he'd hurt Mya...though in all honesty, he really didn't understand it. The whole thing wasn't real to him, somehow. How could he have screwed up so badly?

It was almost as if someone else had been in control of his body. Maybe Yancey was right and he didn't deserve to have a mate. But Mya *was* his mate. That was neither here nor there right this second because his father…shit. His father would kill him and he'd never have to worry about this or anything else again. How had his life spiraled so far out of control in just one day?

Chapter 10

Eyes fixed on his dangling hands, Lakon thought back over the last week with Mya, and then further, to the first day he'd seen her. Actually, it had been night—he'd never forget that night that he and Yancey caught the brother and sister pair playing around with the lighting. Sure, he'd seen her before that but hadn't really taken especial note of her. How stupid was that? He'd had a goddess in his midst, a beautiful-smelling, mate type goddess and he hadn't noticed her for a year or more. Not only that, but he'd had her in his arms, in his life, and chased her away.

What the hell was wrong with him? Did he have some sort of psychological problem where he sabotaged his chances for happiness or something? That didn't' sound like him. He'd always been a selfish bastard, though. There was no denying that. The sight of his brother holding Mya against his body had made Lakon nuts. Crazy, wild, nuts.

Yancey was angry at him because he couldn't control himself. He'd hurt Mya because he hadn't been able to control his animal instincts. He was a werewolf, damn it! Of course he had animal instincts. And with a grandmother who was full wolf, it just made his instincts stronger.

What should he do? Lakon shot to his feet, pacing to the window. With a restless twitch he flipped the curtain aside and then let it drop. He didn't care what was out there. He strode back to the couch and turned, restlessly circling the room. He had to do something— anything, just something! He was going to go stir crazy if he didn't do something. He had to fix this mess with his mate. He'd worry about the rest of the family later. Mya was out there somewhere. He needed to talk to Myles. No doubt he knew where his sister was.

To hell with this! Lakon couldn't take it anymore, he had to get away. Away from his thoughts, away from this hotel room where he's made love with Mya and then where he'd hurt her. With a growl, he wrenched open the door and charged out, slamming it behind him as he went.

There were cabs lined up in front of the hotel and it was only a matter of slowing down long enough to open a car door and slide in before he was on his way to the edge of the city. There could possibly be parks or something but he needed to run, to fight. No doubt he'd find what he was looking for in the Uwharrie forest.

With a last suspicious glance and a very large gratuity, the driver finally pulled away, leaving Lakon outside of a shuttered information center long after closing time. The most complicated part of this little endeavor would be where to put his clothing, though this wasn't the first time the situation had come up. Normally, of course, there was a modicum of planning involved. Lakon couldn't be bothered to worry about such things right now. He had energy and anger to work off, no doubt camouflaged shame, but he'd deal with that later.

Finally finding a hard to reach nook to hide his clothing, Lakon quickly stripped and shifted into his werewolf form. It felt good, flowing, like coming home. Sometimes he felt more natural as a man, but just as often, he felt like he belonged in fur instead of denim and leather.

Wasting no time, he slipped through the underbrush at the side of the trail, nose to the vine tangled ground, looking for prey. Maybe he'd eat, maybe not, but he needed to hunt.

So many scents coming from all directions, Lakon felt overwhelmed for just a moment, then he realized something. There'd been a fight here, some kind of a conflict of territory. Local dogs, feral apparently, and then there was the scent of bobcats, along with that, some other animal, something that wasn't man but didn't belong- -he couldn't' find a name for whatever it was, but it was a predator. In wolf form, his thoughts didn't always work exactly as they did in man form. And with a grandparent who was a wolf, he really had to fight his primal nature. On two legs, he'd name something a bear or a cow, but on four, it was predator or prey. Oh, sure, he could tell the difference if he wanted to, but he didn't right now. He wanted to think like an animal. It was easier. Much easier.

* * * *

Mya was glad to be walking in the mountains. She had always believed that she belonged here, outside, in the green grass and tall trees. This was where she truly felt at home.

Right now, she was heading toward the home of her friend, Sandy Eiderhook, who lived in Blowing Rock, North Carolina. She thought about how she'd come here after Myles' big injury six years before. That time she'd sold herself and her virginity to a hospital administrator for the price of her brother's treatment, drugs and two months of home care.

The last time she'd visited Sandy was three years ago. She'd been working for a veterinarian who was a wildlife expert. She'd loved that job and had hoped that she could learn a lot from the man. She'd learned quite a bit about wildlife and she'd learned a little something about defending herself.

After a year of working for him and soaking up all the knowledge he could give her, her employer had decided that she was just playing hard to get. The man she'd worked for and trusted nearly succeeded in raping her. She'd escaped and her ex-boss had tried to follow her. That was when Mya ran to Sandy.

They'd been living in South Carolina then and Myles had been working for a local newspaper. Her foot and leg had been injured and getting to Sandy's hadn't been easy.

She'd understood how hard it had been on Myles. He'd understood how hard it had been on her. Now, brother and sister were on something closer to equal footing. She was hiking in the mountains to find peace with herself. He'd stayed behind because he chose to, not because he didn't have any other choice.

Mya flatly refused to think about Lakon Montgomery. Well, she wouldn't think about him on purpose or in detail. He was the constant ache in her heart. If she didn't feel him there, she felt him in her throbbing shoulder.

Looking across the field, she realized that she was nearing her old friend's house. When she and Myles had been barely sixteen, Sandy had helped them with Myles's treatment. Ultimately, they'd had to move on and work in the city but Sandy had helped them in that as well.

With her natural affinity for animals, Mya had helped Sandy, too. He'd worked with animals for many years but had decided, late in life, to go to school to become a licensed veterinarian. Mya had assisted him from time to time during his internship. She'd also helped him study when he came to the restaurant where she had been a waitress. They'd kept in touch, loosely.

Mya approached his back door and heard him talking to someone. Sandy wasn't a young man and he wasn't married. Neither did Sandy watch television. She didn't want to interrupt him and she didn't want to draw attention to herself.

She knocked on the door. "Sandy!" she called out.

The door wrenched open and there he was, a sight for sore eyes, to be sure. Tall and thin with a long, white ponytail pulled back from his face. Mya was so glad to see him, she felt her eyes sting.

"Mya Brooks! Is that really you?" He reached out and then stepped back, holding the door open wide. Sandy would know better than to grab her. He beamed at her from the doorway, waiting for her to enter.

Mya knew that he was fifty or sixty but he still acted like he was in his twenties. A glance to the side showed a weight bench just beyond his mud sink. Some people never really aged. Now that she was older, she wished she'd fallen for him.

"Hiya, Sandy. Did I hear you talking to someone?"

"How's my little English rose? Look how much you've grown up! You sure got a handle on that beautiful voice. I saw you on television the other day!"

"That's wonderful, Sandy. Did you say you've got company?" she persisted.

"No, madam, I did not. And I don't have a famous singer turning up at my doorstep for no apparent reason, do I?" They'd always been straight with each other. Now seemed like a good time to follow that tradition.

"No, not for no reason."

"Where's your brother? More importantly, where's your boyfriend?" Sandy demanded, leading her into his kitchen.

"Myles is in the hospital. He's at Duke getting something done to, or maybe *about*, his genes." She gave her old friend a watery smile. It had been a long day and a long night before that. She was so very glad to be safe at Sandy's house finally.

*

Mik Montgomery sat in the laundry room off of his old friend's kitchen. They'd been enjoying a good argument over a game of chess when Sandy had exclaimed, "Good Lord, I don't believe it!" On the heels of that, he'd demanded, "When's the last time you've spoken to Lakon?"

Before Mik could answer, Sandy had shoved him into the laundry room and bade him to stay there, be quiet, and listen. Mik wasn't sure why, but he was listening hard. Oh, he understood being shoved out of sight. After all, he was a very large wolf that talked. Or at least, that was what most people would see. Even if he tried to just play the tame wolf for Sandy's guests, he knew he was frightening to those who didn't know him. He was simply too large not to be scary. His thoughts were interrupted by the change in Sandy's tone as he spoke to the young woman at his door.

"Let me guess, he's being treated by a Livingston or a Montgomery?"

That got Mik's attention. So did the girl's wariness when Sandy asked the question.

"Why would you suspect that, Sandy? You know, it's getting late, really, I should be going…"

"Sit down and tell me what's going on, young lady!" Sandy barked, pressing her into a chair with her back to the laundry room. "You gotta know Lakon Montgomery is from this part of the country if you're sleeping with him!"

Mik was taken aback. Sandy had called this girl a famous singer. Never one for television or even radio, Mik counted on his family to keep him updated on what they were doing and who it was they were doing things with. Was this the woman his son had called him about? Lakon had been so taken with this girl. He'd cared so much and been so sincere. Why was she so far away from Lakon now? He needed to call his son and find out. Although he had a feeling he'd know very soon if he just kept quiet.

"Okay, um, give me a minute. Got coffee?" Her voice sounded oddly high.

Mik heard Sandy bustling around making coffee. He pushed the laundry room door open a little more. Finally, Sandy set a cup of coffee in front of himself and his little guest, settling near her.

"Mya, the last time you came calling, something bad had happened to you. In fact, every time you come calling that's true. Now you talk to me, girl." Sandy sounded gruff to Mik.

"The short answer is, I was bitten by a big dog," Mya told Sandy. Mik sat up straight.

"You mean…You don't mean…" Sandy was having trouble asking the question.

"I mean a very large lycanthrope became angry with me and bit me. It needs treatment," she said steadily.

"He really bit you?" Sandy was incredulous. The girl nodded. "Let me see it."

Mik was grateful that the laundry room was immediately behind the kitchen table. He couldn't see her face but he was beginning to have a terrible feeling in the pit of his stomach.

"Okay," she breathed, unbuttoning her shirt.

The young woman sat up straight in her chair and let the shirt drop from her right shoulder. It was obvious that she could barely move the shoulder and the swollen area around it was purple and green. The puncture wounds might have been infected.

"Jesus, God," Sandy breathed. He gingerly touched her swollen shoulder. "Lakon Montgomery did this to you, child?" Sandy asked in a voice just above a whisper.

Mik couldn't see it that well. He didn't *want* to see it if the tone of Sandy's voice was a good barometer of how bad the injury was.

"It's a whole thing, Sandy," she said, carefully.

"I'd really like to hear the whole thing, otherwise, I might find a way to kill the son of a bitch in his sleep – or wide awake…" Sandy began bustling around, probably trying to assemble things that could make Mya's shoulder feel better. Mik came out of the small room and looked in horror at the girl's shoulder.

"I'm not saying he shouldn't have – I dunno, not done that or something. But I think it started with his brother…" Mya was trying to be fair.

"You're gonna have to be more specific, Mya," Sandy said through gritted teeth. Mik didn't need his werewolf senses to tell him how angry his old friend was.

"We were at the Amphitheatre in Raleigh and Riker came out of nowhere. He was all over me and I felt like a tasty bone. I was too scared to move. He made Lakon real mad. After that, things just got worse and worse."

"What aren't you telling me, Mya?" Sandy demanded.

"I just can't Sandy. That's just… I can't okay?" She began to cry but managed to get control of herself pretty quickly. "I'm here because I need your help and I need some space. Can you make that feel better at all?"

"I'll help you. I can make it feel better. While I treat you…" Mik moved around the chair. "I want you to meet someone."

As soon as the girl saw Mik, she shot to her feet. "You're one of *them*, aren't you?"

Mik's heart dropped. His son was in love with a girl who couldn't accept that he was a werewolf. She must know, after all. *Them* spoken in just that inflection could only mean werewolf. If Lakon had caused this injury, he guessed he couldn't blame her.

"You're a *Montgomery*, aren't you?" she breathed, backing away from him. She used the same tone one might use to say "child molester" or "serial killer". He was stunned.

"Mya?" he asked, incredulous.

"You can't take me back. I don't want to be hurt anymore. Poor Bethany. I hope they don't hurt her, too…"

Mik was taken aback. The poor little thing was shaking like a leaf. She was a wreck.

"Honey, sit down. I swear I won't try to take you anywhere. Here, have some coffee." Mik tried to sooth Mya, nudging the coffee toward her with his nose. "Sandy, put something in that coffee to help her calm down."

"You are, aren't you? You're a Montgomery." She looked at Mik accusingly. "If I had to fall in love with a dog, why'd it have to be a mean one?"

Sandy poured some whiskey into her coffee and laid an ice pack on her shoulder. Gently he eased her back into the chair. "I'm gonna give you a cortisone shot in a little bit. I wanna clean that out some first, but just calm down, okay?"

She turned her reproachful eyes to Sandy. "I thought I could trust you, Sandy." Her eyes filled with tears. Mik wanted nothing more than to kill his sons right then. Both of them, slowly.

"Mya, I promise I won't hurt you or try to take you anywhere. I won't tell anybody where you are, I promise you on the lives of my grandsons."

"You're not going to change into a big, mean human man now?" she asked him.

"What you see is what you get, young lady. I'm a werewolf but I don't transform. My mother was *Canis lupus occidentalis*, a Rocky Mountain Wolf. My father was a werewolf." He hoped all this made sense to her. She didn't seem as hysterical as she had before.

Mya nodded, her reluctant curiosity taking over for a minute. "So werewolves can marry regular wolves *or* people?"

"Yes, honey." Mik breathed a sigh of relief. She was much calmer now. "I want to understand, Mya. You're not upset about werewolves in general, just Montgomery werewolves?"

She looked at him with unfathomable hurt in her eyes and nodded. "I had to think about it a while and it *is* mind-boggling. I thought of Lakon as my husband. Wouldn't he be mad if I was really a – a, I don't know – a bird or something? What if I kept it from him and he didn't know?" She was angry but there were tears of sorrow in her eyes.

Mik moved closer to her and sat down in front of her. "He should have told you, honey." Mik nodded.

"Did your wife know you were a werewolf before you... slept together?" She blushed, maybe because it was such a personal question.

"She did know. Elke is a werewolf, too. But she can transform and I can't. She knew that too but it didn't seem important to her at first. Later it bothered her. She's gotten past it now." He wasn't sure why he was sharing such things with her but it was time someone from the Montgomery pack showed this woman some trust.

"At least she had the information up front."

Sandy got up and began cleaning Mya's bite wound since she'd calmed down. Her shoulder was exposed but the flannel shirt she wore covered the rest of her upper body.

"Anyway, it turns out, being with Lakon, I know lots of werewolves who aren't Montgomerys. I only realized that last night, of course. But none of *them* have ever hurt me or acted as if they might. Riker and Lakon have," she sniffed again, obviously fighting to keep from crying.

"Tell me exactly what happened, Mya. Start from the beginning." Mik was determined to get to the bottom of things.

"We were at the Alltel Pavilion, a big enclosed amphitheatre, and I was halfway up the stands and heading down them, toward the stage. Lakon was on the stage and there was this beautiful blonde woman with him. He had his head near her tummy so I could see her face. I stopped walking toward them because I was trying to figure out why she was so familiar to me. I knew I'd never met her."

Mya stopped to take a drink of her coffee and winced when Sandy injected the cortisone and placed a hot compress on her injury.

"That had to be Bet, right?" Mik asked, encouraging her to go on.

"Yes, Bethany," Mya agreed. "Anyway, while I was standing there, a man, Riker Montgomery, came up behind me and put his arm around me. He was pressed against me and pulled my head aside so he could put his mouth on my neck."

She stopped talking, taking great gulps of air. Mik rubbed his forehead against her side in comfort and she lowered her head. It took a great deal of effort, but he somehow managed not to respond to her story by growling.

"He was licking me and stuff." Mya continued her account of the event with a delicate shudder. "I tried to get away and he growled at me. He wouldn't let me go. I asked him to but he wouldn't. Lakon came and the two of them started snarling at each other." Her voice was a little higher now. Tears shimmered in her eyes. "They were growling and in each other's faces and I was stuck between them. If Bethany hadn't come and gotten me, I don't know what would have happened. But the rest of the day, Lakon was kind of angry. Then, that night..." She jumped up, and shook her head back and forth, the hovering tears now streaming down her face.

"I have to go to the bathroom." She bolted from the room.

When she came out many minutes later, she was much calmer. Mik and Sandy were talking quietly.

"Feel better, honey?" Mik asked her. "You look pretty tired."

Sandy had finished treating her wound before she had fled the room. "I *am* tired. I left Lakon last night in the middle of the night. I didn't get much sleep. I know he probably won't realize I was gone till sometime today."

Mik decided to let her skip that part of the story for the time being. "Perhaps you should lie down for awhile, Mya. I was already visiting with Sandy, so we'll just go on with our visit. We won't bother you while you get some rest."

She looked from man to werewolf and back again, reluctance stamped across her features. "I-I don't know. I usually just take the couch and..."

"You can have the sofa in the den, child," Sandy offered, cutting her off. "It's nicer than the other one, and it's dark and cool in there."

Mya's desire to resist was clearly at war with the exhaustion of the last day and night and finally, the exhaustion won. She nodded once, sharply, and then followed Sandy down the hall.

After a brief internal struggle, Mik decided to wait a while to call home. The girl needed rest and he needed to calm down. He and Sandy could chat or maybe he would go for a walk. Any talking he did to a family member right now, even Elke, would result in raised voices at the very least. With a sigh, Mik lowered himself to the floor and rested his head between his paws. Maybe he needed a little nap, too.

Chapter 11

Mya was dozing when she heard someone dialing a phone. She heard the sound of it ringing and realized it was on speakerphone.

"Hello?" a woman's voice answered.

"Hello, love, how are you?" It was the deep baritone voice of that wolf – werewolf, Mik.

"When are you coming home, Mik? The boys are pretty upset." The woman sounded a little upset to Mya.

"I'm pretty upset, too, Elke." growled Mik.

"Lakon said his mate found out he's a werewolf and she's afraid of him!" Elke said tearfully.

This was Mik's wife and Lakon's mother! Mya held herself very still on the couch, curious about their conversation. Would Mik tell his wife that he knew where she was? Could she trust Mik not to lead Lakon to her?

"Lakon's mate isn't afraid of werewolves, love, she's afraid of Montgomery werewolves," he rumbled angrily.

"That's a switch, isn't it?" the woman responded breathlessly.

"I'll ponder the irony of that on the way home, Elke. When I get there, I want both those boys sitting on the porch waiting for me with their tails between their legs."

"Mik?" The woman, Elke, sounded surprised and scared.

"If they make me go into the city to rip a strip off their pelts, I'm gonna make both Mya *and* Bethany widows. You tell them that. I never thought I could be so ashamed of my own sons. Never. I'll be home in a few hours."

"Mik, are you okay?"

"I'm feeling pretty low right now, Elke. I love you. I'll be home soon."

Mya heard the dial tone and waited. She listened as Mik and Sandy talked to each other.

"Take care of her, Sandy. I'll call tomorrow night. I don't like keeping a man away from his mate but I gave her my word. After what he did, I don't know that he's a fit mate anyway."

The werewolf sounded so sad and dejected to her. Mya wanted to go in there and comfort him. For some reason, she knew she could trust the old wolf.

"Mik." She called his name softly.

She heard him padding into the room and around the couch toward her, his nails clicking lightly on the worn wood flooring. She'd been lying on her left side and now she sat up, cross-legged. Her shoulder was throbbing in time with her heart and she couldn't remember the last time she'd hurt so much.

"Mik?" she said again. He stepped onto the couch and sat down at her side, looking down at her. "I'm sorry about all this, Mik." She felt the tears gather in her eyes again.

The old wolf placed his head next to hers in a hug. "I'm sorry, too, honey."

She wrapped her good arm around him and gave him a squeeze. He rested his chin on the crown of her head and patted her carefully with his large paw.

"I wish I could make it all better, honey.".

"I wish you could, too," she answered sadly.

"Stay here with Sandy and rest a bit. Maybe things will look better in a day or so."

She didn't answer him. She was crying softly. He stepped off the couch and she lay back down on her side, bringing her knees to her chest. Mik tugged a throw from the back of the couch and covered her. He licked her cheek and let her stroke his head and neck until she fell asleep.

* * * *

Lakon and Riker sat on the porch of their parent's home occasionally indulging in desultory conversation, but for the most part, they didn't speak at all. Both men were in wolf form.

Lakon had just opened his mouth to say something to his brother when a large silver wolf rocketed onto the porch and grabbed Riker by the upper back. Before the brown wolf could react, the older wolf, Mik, tossed him across the yard and was on him again.

Mik immediately grabbed him by the side and tossed him into the air. As soon as he could move, Riker rolled to his back, exposing his underbelly in supplication. Lakon could hear what his father said from his vantage on the porch.

"She struggled and you growled at her," Mik rumbled angrily. "You held her against her will, you scared her, she asked you to stop and you growled at her!" Mik grabbed Riker's throat and shook him, dropping his son before he did lasting damage.

Lakon could see the fear in his brother's eyes. Mik was a frightening sight with his hackles raised and his ears straight up. His lips were curled in an angry snarl and drool dripped from his fangs. His yellow eyes glowed menacingly in the dark night.

"You think it's funny to scare the hell out of an innocent girl just to get a rise out of your brother? *Do you?*"

"Dad, I'm sorry," Riker didn't sound like the pack alpha just now. "I didn't know he'd react like that…"

"You're his twin, you damned well *did* know! You didn't think beyond torturing your brother, did you? It never occurred to you that you were scaring the hell out of an innocent human female, did it? Didn't think about any other consequences your actions could cause, did you? I'm ashamed of you, son. Get out of my sight."

Riker scrambled backward and slunk away, shame and humiliation in every line of his body.

Mik moved slowly toward his remaining son who stepped off the porch, shaking but resolute – almost eager to take his medicine.

"You wanna know what I just left?" he snarled bitterly at his son. "Let me tell you!"

Lakon stood straight, determined that he'd be a man about this. Nothing his father had in store for him could be worse than what had already happened he was sure. His father's words changed his mind.

"I just left a sweet, innocent woman, who cried herself to sleep. I tucked her in and put her to sleep after *she* tried to comfort *me*. I was feeling upset you see, because my sons had hurt her so badly. She told me that *she* was sorry about all this – as if *she* were somehow to blame."

Mik moved into his son's face, teeth bared, snarling. "*She's* sorry. She hugged me, too." He took a breath, his lip curled, still drooling and menacing. "She hugged me with her left arm because she can't move her right arm. *At all.*"

He grabbed Lakon by the large muscle above his right front leg and flipped him to ground, slamming the air from his lungs. Once again, he moved into his son's face. Lakon rolled upright again.

"You want to tell me why she's so afraid of Montgomerys? Not werewolves, just *Montgomery* werewolves."

He grabbed Lakon's neck and shook him hard, lifting him from the ground and flinging him several feet away. Winded once again, Lakon lay on his back now, as his brother had. His stomach, chest and privates were exposed in submission.

"Why don't you just cut to the part where you bit her? What else did you do to her, son? Anything you can admit to your old dad? She ran from the room, hysterical, when we got to that part of the story…" Mik was shaking with anger. "I just told your mate that things would look better in a day or two. How badly did I lie to that sweet little girl, son?"

Lakon closed his eyes. "Oh, God, Dad. I love her so much. I can't believe I did anything to hurt her. I wish I could take it all back. I just don't know what happened. I never thought I could ever do anything to hurt her…"

Lakon didn't try to stem the few tears trickling from his eyes. He wished his father would finish the job and rip his throat out. He deserved nothing less. He'd thought he couldn't feel any worse but he did. He definitely did.

Chapter 12

It had been three days since Mya had arrived at Sandy's house. She was beginning to feel antsy and knew it was time to go. The fact that it was raining just confirmed for her that tonight was a good night to leave.

She knew that her scent would be harder to track after the rain. She'd made arrangements with Sandy to pick up necessities occasionally for her little hideaway. She didn't know how long she'd be gone but she made sure that Sandy could get in touch with Myles, if need be.

With her bag packed and all her supplies wrapped in plastic, there was only one thing left for Mya to do. The old wolf had been honest with her. She'd be honest with him. With Sandy's help, she called Mik.

* * * *

"Hello?" Elke answered the phone as usual, when it rang. "Yes, he is. Just a moment." Mik heard the uncertainty in his wife's voice, but it didn't register.

"Mik, the phone's for you." He raised a brow but didn't remark on it. He seldom got phone calls.

He glanced over at his sons staring morosely into the fire as he reached for the button on the speakerphone.

"Mik Montgomery here," he said quietly. Riker glanced over at him but didn't speak. Lakon continued to look into the flickering flames.

"Mik?" a sweet, mildly accented voice said. "It's Mya."

Lakon bolted upright, spilling his coffee. Mik gave a low warning growl.

"Mik, are you alright? Did I call at a bad time?" She sounded to Mik like she was eager to end the call.

"I'm fine, honey, just spilled some coffee, that's all," he improvised quickly.

"Are you burned? A teabag or some lavender oil will make you feel better."

"It's okay Mya, just a little spill. How are you? How's your arm?" he asked in concern.

"Um, Mik, I-I called to say goodbye and thank you for trying to make me feel better. I'm leaving in a few minutes." Her voice was halting and he could tell she was fighting her emotions. Lakon stared at the phone, gripping the arms of his chair tightly.

"Are you going to see your brother, Mya?" Mik asked, knowing in his gut that she wasn't.

"No, I'm not going to see Myles. I'm heading into the mountains."

"Mya, honey…" He took a deep breath, shaking his head at Lakon who opened his mouth to speak. "It's raining out there now."

"I know, Mik," she said gently.

"You can barely use your right arm, honey."

"I know, Mik," she repeated, even more gently.

"Don't you…" he wanted to ask if she didn't trust him to keep his word but didn't know if he had the right to ask. "Mya, Lakon…"

"Mik, I just need to be on my own right now. Please don't make it more than that." He heard her take a deep breath. "Could you do something for me?"

"Anything honey." His son stared at him, pleading.

"Just take care of him for me, okay?" He could hear her voice break though she cleared her throat to hide it.

"Do you think you'll ever forgive him, Mya?" Mik hoped he could move the couple toward reconciliation. His son's eyes were breaking his heart.

"I forgave him right away, Mik. It's just… Forgetting what he did takes longer. I have to go." He heard a rustling movement and then the sound of a door opening and closing.

"Mik?" It was Sandy.

"How could you let her go, Sandy?" Mik growled at his old friend. "Sit down, son!" he barked at Lakon.

"She's an adult, man. I can't sit on her. She'll keep in touch with Myles and me. We've been down this road before."

"Why didn't you call me sooner? I could've been there, tracked her… something!" Mik barked.

"Look, maybe I should've seen the signs. She only ever stays long enough for me to patch her up a little. After that, she goes off into the woods and licks her wounds."

"How's her shoulder? Does she have supplies? How is she, Sandy?" To Lakon, he said, "Son, ten minutes won't make a difference. Sandy may know where she's going."

"Gentlemen, don't sit there thinking that you're going to just track her. That wildlife expert that was harassing her came after her.

89

Didn't ever find her. There was plenty of evidence that *she* knew he was there. I couldn't find her either but she did keep in touch."

The two men finished their phone call and hung up.

"Dad," Lakon choked, "We have to go find her. *I* have to go find her."

"Son, go if you think it'll help. Nobody's better than Sandy. By the time you get there, even if you drive, she'll be long gone. But go. Sandy lives in Blowing Rock." He turned to his other son. "Riker, you go see Maisie at Duke in a couple of days. See if she can get you in to see that brother."

* * * *

Riker entered Myles' dim hospital room and saw a very fit looking young man seemingly asleep on the bed. As he stood inside the door, debating the best way to awaken this young man, Drs. Maisie and Jane Montgomery and Dr. Abel Livingston entered the room.

"Riker," fawned Dr. Livingston, "I just heard you were here. What can we do for you, sir?"

"Have you come to check on Myles progress?" asked Dr. Jane Montgomery.

Before Riker could answer, the young man in the bed spoke up. "I don't give a raging rat's arse *why* he's here. I didn't invite him and he can go now."

Maisie stepped forward. "Myles, he's our Alpha. You can't talk to him like that."

"Maisie, he's *your* Alpha, not mine. I can talk to him any damned way I want to. If he wants to fight me for Alpha of the Brooks clan, he can wait until you guys are done screwing around with me, or he can damn well come ahead. I don't much give a toss right now."

"Myles, your sister…"

"My sister is not, at this time, mated with a Montgomery according to our customs. Neither she, nor I, since we are not werewolves, feel inclined to change that right this minute."

"Myles!" Maisie was shocked, as were the other two doctors in the room.

"Mr. Brooks is correct. We are both Alphas, since he is the head of his family, and I need to speak with him. You may all leave." Riker decided it was time to step in.

As the doctors filed out, Riker stared at the young human male in the bed. He was very muscular. Even though he obviously suffered from a serious health problem, he was not weak and he was not a man to be trifled with. In spite of the fact that he was only twenty-three years old, Myles Brooks was a grown man and definitely Alpha material.

"Have you changed your mind about mating with Maisie?" Riker asked him.

"I don't believe I've ever committed one way or another about doing anything with Maisie. We've never even gone on a proper date. Not that it's any of your affair..." Myles apparently still felt very hostile towards Riker.

The older man let out a sigh. "Look, obviously, I'm here about your sister. We're all very worried about her."

"Bit late," Myles grumbled. Riker's eyes flashed gold, but he didn't respond. "She's fine. Left Sandy's four days ago. Her shoulder's slightly better. She saw a red fox the other day."

"How do you know all that?" Riker asked. Had she called her brother? They monitored phone calls in and out of here pretty well, especially under the current circumstances. How had they missed that?

Myles held up a newspaper and showed it to him. Pointing to a classified ad, Myles explained, "We have a code we use." Rising from the bed, he paced over to the window and looked out.

Riker sat down on the edge of a chair near the window. "Look, man. I'm sorrier than I can say about the way I acted and my part in what happened between Mya and Lakon. I antagonized my brother by hanging all over your sister and acting like a fool."

He looked down at his hands for a minute. Myles looked over at him, and then turned back to the window.

"Mya has been abused by large men in the past," he said. "You scared the shit out of her." Myles continued looking straight ahead.

"My dad has been a friend of Sandy's for years. He was there the other day when Mya showed up. He got your sister to tell him what happened. She showed him her shoulder."

Myles looked at Riker steadily, waiting. "Dad had us waiting there when he got back home."

Myles lifted a brow but still said nothing. Riker glanced up and saw the three pack members standing outside the door looking through its window. Myles turned his back to the window and focused on Riker.

Riker looked up at Myles again. He could feel the heat in his face.

"Dad kicked my ass real good. Both of us." He closed his eyes and then looked back at Myles.

"Wish I'd been there," Myles said.

"He did a thorough job," Riker told him, pulling off his shirt.

Myles should clearly be able to see the bruising around his throat and, when Riker turned, on his back. The bruising at his ribcage looked especially painful, because, Riker thought, it *was* especially painful.

Miles seemed to be fighting a grin. He lost. Riker couldn't help it, he grinned too.

"Lakon can hardly walk on all fours. Looks like a lame dog when he's in wolf form. Dad damned near killed him. Guess he nearly killed us both. He looks worse than me."

"Your dad must be big and mean to mop the floor with you two giant blokes. Guess you let him…"

"Hell no, we didn't *let* Dad do anything. The old man beat the shit out of me before I ever even realized he was in the neighborhood. Lakon thought he'd be a man about it and face the music. He won't be that stupid again."

Riker pulled out a picture. It showed an enormous silver, brown and blonde wolf sitting between Riker and Lakon. The wolf was seated on his haunches on the floor while the two men stood on either side. The wolf's head came to the top of each man's ribcage.

Myles whistled low.

"My grandmother was a Rocky Mountain Wolf and my grandfather was a Were," Riker explained. "He spent a great deal of time in wolf form, as you can imagine…Anyway, Dad can't transform but he talks the same as we do. I guess you'd find it odd."

"No odder than anything else, or anyone else I've met so far, I expect," Myles allowed with an ironic nod.

Riker laughed. Coming to his feet, Riker extended his hand to Myles. After a pause, Myles shook it. Riker chuckled and nodded his head toward the door. Myles laughed, too. The relief on the faces of the three doctors on the other side of the window was comical.

Chapter 13

The Livingston Care Facility orderly didn't think it was such a big deal to let Auggie Livingston stay in the Rec. Room an extra hour. Sure, he'd be mingling with a larger crowd of patients than usual. In fact, these patients didn't really seem mentally off at all. Neither did Auggie, to tell the truth.

August Livingston had done him a good turn by advising him on a legal matter. Besides, he was tired of hearing about Riker and Lakon Montgomery, too. His mate and his sisters all thought they were so manly and hot. *Grrr.*

He smiled at Auggie as he left the room. Engrossed in conversation with two other Weres, Auggie looked up and smiled back at him. Whatever else anyone said about him, August Livingston had class.

* * * *

"They had some kind of a fight, that's all I know. Rumor has it that she's in the mountains around here somewhere." The speaker, Gil, was a cousin of Auggie's old friend and assistant, Roland.

Gil and his sister were roadies for the *great* Lakon Montgomery. The young man had also produced a towel that Mya Brooks had used to wipe her face after a concert. It seemed that Gil's sister had hoped that Lakon Montgomery would choose her to be his mate. Thanks to a woman scorned, all three men had Mya's scent. Auggie smirked. He'd been right—Mya Brooks did smell lovely.

They didn't really need her scent, though. Auggie knew that all he really needed was Lakon Montgomery's scent. They would follow it from Lakon's home straight to his mate.

The Montgomery's were so sloppy. It would never occur to Lakon that Auggie would escape from this facility. The co-Alpha would think nothing of leaving his lovely human mate alone at some point.

Auggie could wait. He was a very patient man. For now, his focus was on escaping at just the right time. He'd use the same orderly to grant him a special favor. Something small – Auggie would ask to be alone in the library during visiting day.

Nobody ever visited August Livingston – he wasn't allowed visitors. He *was* allowed to be in the library alone. That was the only place he could be left without supervision. The library just happened to share a bathroom with the visitor area.

In two weeks, two Weres from a different pack would come in and pretend to visit Roland. They'd switch places with Auggie and his trusted assistant. By the time the orderlies and nurses figured out what happened, Auggie and Roland would be long gone.

* * * *

Lakon kept coming back to the wide stream that was five miles north of Sandy's place. He hadn't caught Mya's scent yet, but he knew she'd been there. She'd even left Sandy a note and picked up some provisions he'd left for her. It had been nearly three weeks since she'd left him.

He moved into a thick stand of trees and sat down. Obviously, she was masking her scent somehow. What was she doing? Something was nagging at him, but what? He walked back to the area around the stream.

Slowly, he moved away from the stream just letting his nose do the work. There! *A scent that didn't belong...What was it? Buck in rut! Gotcha!* With a relieved sigh, Lakon headed into the woods, following the out-of-season scent.

He saw Mya from nearly two hundred yards away. He got as close as he dared and watched her as she walked. He'd found her den – it was a small cabin hidden in thick trees and bordered by underbrush on two sides.

When she was almost there, he circled around and positioned himself between her and the cabin and waited. Her movements had been pretty careful as she approached, making him wonder if she was being exceptionally cautious. Did she fear that he was tracking her?

As soon as she looked up and saw him in the clearing between her position and the door, she stopped short. For a long time, she stood, just looking at him. After several minutes, she looked all around but apparently didn't find whatever it was she was looking for. He had no doubt she was hoping he just wouldn't be there the next time she looked, and he refused to disappear. They *had* to work this out.

She trudged forward until finally, she was within a few feet of him. She looked so sad and weary. He approached her and gently took her backpack in his teeth. Her eyes filled with tears, but she let go of it and let him take it from her.

They walked a few feet and she stopped, looking at him quizzically. "You're hurt?" she asked softly, evidently noticing his slight limp.

"Not really," he answered through the fabric of her bag.

He didn't want to go into all that now. *How could she worry about him and his injuries in light of her own?* She opened the cabin door and he limped slightly going in, earning him another hard look from her.

Once inside, she walked to a cupboard and pulled out a pair of his sweatpants and one of his shirts. She put them in front of him.

"I figure you're probably not wearing anything under all that fur," she said. "I'll start the fire."

He was glad to transform and put some clothes on. He knew she brought the clothes for herself and not him, but he was pleased that she had them. As soon as he pulled the pants on, he moved over to her and began adding wood to the fire. He didn't bother with the shirt.

When she heard him approach, she moved away, pretending that she had something else she needed to do. He filled a kettle with water and hung it on a hook near the fire.

When he looked over at her, he saw her shaking in silent sobs. He moved up behind her, not being too quiet about it, and gently turned her face into his chest, gathering her against him. He lifted her and carried her to sit on the thick rug near the fire.

Holding her on his lap, he wrapped her tight in his arms and rocked her, resting his cheek against her hair. He could think of nothing to say that wasn't ridiculously inadequate, so he kept silent.

Finally, her sobs subsided. He adjusted her in his arms and began unbuttoning her flannel shirt. Mya froze instantly.

"I'm not going to hurt you, Mya, I promise," he swore, stopping his movements.

"Lakon, don't," she whispered "I-I don't want you to see it."

"I have to see it and take care of it if I can, baby."

He eased the soft flannel from her left arm and then, carefully, from her right arm. Under the shirt, she wore a long-sleeved thermal shirt and he carefully began removing that, too.

.Her eyes were closed when he carefully tugged the left sleeve from her arm and lifted the thermal shirt over her head. He ignored her bare breasts as he began to expose her right shoulder.

His breath caught when he saw the angry purple and red bite-shaped wound with four clear punctures from his canine teeth. No wonder she hadn't tried to put on a bra. It was obvious that there was muscle and tendon damage. Every move must be painful to her right now.

"Mya, baby, we have to have a doctor look at that. You might need surgery or something." He was so completely ashamed of himself. Humans simply didn't heal like werewolves did. He should have known better—should have *behaved* better.

She hung her head and didn't say anything. Lakon lowered his mouth to her injured shoulder and kissed it, lathing it with his tongue. She looked up at him, her eyes filled with pain and fear.

Arms around her, he eased her down on the fluffy rug and slowly covered her mouth with his, kissing her closed lips gently, lovingly, his tongue sensuously worshiping her mouth. He feasted on her lips, her dimples, her chin, nibbling and licking. When his craving demanded more, he parted her lips, his tongue mating passionately with hers. He wanted her badly, but didn't want to take things too far. She wasn't ready, and truly, neither was he. Too much had happened between them.

As he pulled away slowly, Mya reached up and stroked his cheek with her left hand. Lakon continued to kiss her, brief, lingering kisses. Carefully, he reached down to cup her exposed breasts in his hands, keeping his actions slow and gentle. At first he brushed her nipples with his fingers and then began rolling them between his fingertips. It was hard for him to restrain himself. He could feel his beast eager to claim her, take his mate and make her his own once again.

His hot mouth moved down her throat to her clavicle and down to her breasts, taking one into his mouth and sucking deeply. He nipped at her nipple and then lathed it with his tongue, transferring his attentions to the other nipple and repeating the process.

"Lakon." Her voice sounded fearful and shaky. She pushed against his naked chest.

Lakon raised his head from her breast and tugged her against him, rolling onto his back and cradling her against his chest. He pulled her flannel shirt over her, but he continued to run his hands over the satin skin under it.

"I was so worried, Mya," he confessed. "So afraid I'd never see you, never touch you again." Her head rested against his chest and he stroked her hair.

"Why did you hurt me, Lakon?" she whispered, not lifting her head. He could feel warm tears seeping into the fur of his chest.

He took a deep breath. "I wasn't thinking straight, Mya. You're *my* mate and it just seemed like everyone was threatening that. The more threatened I felt, the more intrusive every other man's actions toward you seemed to be." He took another deep breath. He had to explain this the right way, and be honest. Nothing less than the humbling truth would do. "Riker is my twin brother."

She nodded. "I know that."

"For every wolf, there is one mate and we know when we've found her. It's like an imprint on your soul. Sometimes if a mate dies, there can be another, but almost never."

She nodded against his chest again. "Okay, so far."

"With twins, we're so alike in so many ways that we could, conceivably, have the same mate." He blew out a sigh.

She lifted her bare torso from his, propping herself on her forearms. "Lakon?" He looked up into her whiskey colored eyes.

"What, baby?" he murmured. He wanted her so much. She had to know that.

"Be honest, okay? I won't be mad."

His brow furrowed. "Okay."

"When you first met Bethany, what did you think?" He hadn't expected that.

Honesty. He could do that. That was the whole point of this entire exercise, wasn't it?

"Um, Bethany. Well, she was beautiful. And she smelled damned good." His face and neck began to color. *She wanted honest*... "Yeah, I wanted her."

Mya nodded. "Did you go for her?"

"Huh? Of course not!" How could she ask that?

"How come?" She sounded genuinely curious.

"She was my brother's mate! Riker loved her so much." Why was she asking these questions?

"You told me you loved me the first time we made love." She lay back down on his chest.

"Mya?" He tipped her face to look at him. "Baby, I *do* love you. I love you more than my life. I don't love Bethany the way I love you. I never have, never will. You know that, don't you?"

"I know that your brother loves his wife and she loves him. He was just being stupid." Her eyes filled with tears. "I know you're sorry that you hurt me Lakon. I believe you do love me." She moved her head down a little and turned so that she wasn't looking at him.

"But?" He knew there was a "but". *There's always a "but".*

"How can I trust you not to hurt me again?" Her breath clutched on a sob.

Running his hands up and down her smooth back, he tried to answer her.

"These last three weeks have taught me some important things, baby. I don't think I can explain each thing that I've learned. But I do know that I have to earn your trust back. Will you give me a chance?"

"How do I do that, Lakon? How do I know you won't do this again? What if some guy whistles at me? We work in an industry that…well, guys ogle me all the time. You *know* that."

"Stay with me tonight. Just for tonight. If that goes okay, stay tomorrow, too. Maybe, if enough days and nights go okay, you'll want to stay with me for a week… If I earn your trust again, maybe someday, you'll stay with me for a lifetime?"

"Oh, Lakon." She began to cry again.

"Shhh, baby, it'll be okay. Let's go to bed – to sleep. Maybe we'll be hungry when we wake up." She nodded, still crying silently.

He lifted her and carried her to the narrow bed in the corner. Undressing her and placing her in it, he climbed in behind her and wrapped himself around her. No matter what happened next, he was here with her. There was a chance.

Chapter 14

Myles sat in yet another doctor's office wondering if he'd ever escape back into the real world again. This was another one of Yancey and Lakon's cousins, a Dr. Abel Livingston. Myles imagined that the old, *"Doctor Livingston, I presume"* thing had gotten old quite some time ago. This time, the doctor wasn't alone.

"Myles, you know Riker Montgomery, of course, and this is Mr. Mik Montgomery." Dr. Jane Montgomery and Dr. Abel Livingston introduced the giant wolf.

Myles stood and reached out a hand to Mik. He wasn't sure what the normal protocol was when one met a talking wolf, so he decided to pretend it was all normal to him.

"Pleased to meet you sir." *He's even more formidable in person.*

Mik lifted a large paw and shook Myles hand. "I'm very fond of your sister," he told Myles.

Myles smiled. His life might be out-of-control, surreal, but he could certainly agree on one particular point. "She's easy to love, Mya is."

"I guess you're wondering why I've called you all here today?" Dr. Livingston intoned somberly, and then chuckled. "I've always wanted to say that."

Riker, Mik, and Myles just stared at him unmoving. The doctor cleared his throat.

"Okay, well, simply put there is a way to treat, and essentially, to *cure* Myles's hemophilia," Dr. Livingston explained.

Myles opened his mouth to rebut that, having been told at every given opportunity that there was *not* a way to cure him. But these were the professionals and most likely knew a great many things he did not. He kept his mouth shut and waited for the catch. There was *always* a catch.

"The thing is," said Dr. Montgomery, "either of the principals – that would be you, Myles, or you Mik, um Mr. Montgomery," she cleared her throat again. "Either one of you might object."

"As you know, Myles' disease is worsening somewhat because of several factors. Some of the past treatments he's had have left his autoimmune system weaker, his joints are at risk and infections are even more of a threat than in the past." Dr. Livingston seemed much more comfortable talking about the disease than he was cracking jokes. Myles certainly liked him better that way. "He's deteriorating rapidly."

On the other hand, he really didn't like doctors much at all as a group.

"This is exciting for us for a number of reasons." Dr. Montgomery actually did seem excited, stepping in front of her Livingston counterpart and waving her hands expressively to punctuate her statements. "Generally speaking, werewolves don't get diseases like hemophilia. As geneticists and doctors, we study and work with *all* diseases and disorders that affect genes – even the ones that do not impact our kind. This is an opportunity we've never had before now."

Myles noticed that the other two men stared at the doctors without blinking. He wondered if they were interested or bored stupid. Mik cleared that up for him.

"Cut to the chase Jane, or I'm going to lie down on the floor," he rumbled.

Myles and Riker exchanged looks. It was obvious to Myles that he wasn't the only one in the room fighting not to burst into laughter.

"Um, yes," Dr. Livingston flushed. Jane Montgomery was too embarrassed to speak. "Well, with Mr. Brooks there and his sister both being so closely involved in the family, we, uh, um." He cleared his throat and said in a rush, "Mik, if you want to donate a lot of your blood and let us splice some of your genes with some of his, we think we can cure him."

Myles saw Riker arch a brow. He knew that Mik was as stunned as he was.

"Before we get to the "hows" and "wherefores", let's talk end result," Riker insisted.

Yeah, I wanted to ask that, too! It was all Myles could do to formulate any words at all. It felt like his brains had frozen, right along with his mouth. He took a deep breath and let it out slowly.

"What happens to my body besides no more hemophilia?" Myles finally got out.

"Essentially, you will become lupine but you won't be able to transform like Dr. Livingston, myself and Riker can. To put it plainly, you'll be like the quintessential opposite of Mr. Montgomery," Dr. Montgomery explained, nodding toward Mik.

Myles and Mik looked at each other for a minute. "Um, will I still be able to speak?" *Mik lives in a wolf body but talks, if I'm opposite of him, it's a fair question...*

"We believe so," answered Dr. Livingston. *We believe so? Doctors!*

"Why Dad and not me?" asked Riker.

"You are our second choice, sir, but we feel that your father's biology is more likely to ensure success. We'll need some of your blood for your father, anyway."

"Go out there for a minute," Mik told the doctors, angling his head toward the door. Needless to say, they did. "What do you think, son?" Mik asked Myles.

"I think my future's looking pretty bleak right now," Myles answered. It wasn't as if they hadn't just sat beside him and listened to the same spiel.

Myles decided that he'd either taken leave of his senses or had nothing much left to lose. Either way, this might be the only chance he had left. Mya had said that she loved Lakon. He knew she'd forgive him. As he understood things, Mya and Lakon were basically married as far as the werewolves were concerned, so this was to be Myles' family now and forever. They didn't do the divorce thing, and they took very good care of their families if Riker was to be believed. The jury was still out regarding his opinion of Lakon, but Mya *would* forgive him...well, in that case, Myles might as well officially join the family, too. It might be nice having something like parents and brothers.

"How do you feel about having wolf and werewolf in your system?" Riker asked him.

"You don't have fleas do you?" Myles grinned at Mik.

"No, but I shed a lot," Mik grinned back. "You want another brother, son?" he asked Riker.

"You promise to beat the shit out of him like you did me and Lakon?" Riker grinned and nudged Myles.

"Every single time he deserves it, I'm gonna kick his ass, you bet." The three were grinning at each other as Riker waved the doctors back into the room.

"Before I let either of you mad scientists drag these two into your evil la-*bor*-atory..." Riker looked hard at the doctors, each in turn. "If one of these guys dies? One of you guys dies. Think it over."

"Oh, no, sir. The only danger is to Myles here…" At Riker's arched brow and curled lip, Dr. Livingston continued quickly, "I mean the danger is the same as it was before. No worse."

Riker nodded. The doctor released a relieved sigh.

After another hour of questions and a phone call to Elke, Myles and Mik agreed. They would allow the procedure. Myles excused himself to put his ad in the classified section telling his sister what was up. The treatments began that evening.

* * * *

"So, you're going to do it?"

The question startled Myles out of a fitful doze and he struggled to sit, squinting toward the door. He could see the silhouette of a man in the bright backlight, but was still too sleepy to identify him.

"Hmm?" he asked, trying to orient himself. "'M sorry, do I know you?" he mumbled.

His condition had declined steadily since he'd spoken to the doctors with Riker and Mik. In fact, that consultation, which had taken place four days prior, marked the last reasonably functional day he'd had. Now, his head felt fuzzy and his joints hurt. He was bruised all over, as if someone had diligently poked him with one finger over and over until his skin became a mottled rainbow of dull color.

"It's me, Myles. Yancey," the man identified himself, coming further into the room. "Damn. You look like hell."

"Just close the door," Myles grumbled, "the light hurts my eyes. Everything just feels…like I've been plowed over by a lorry or something."

Yancey moved further into the room, pulling the door closed behind him. "I had no idea. I mean, I knew you had this illness and I saw that bruise the first day but I just didn't know this could happen," he babbled, stepping up to the side of the bed. Reaching out, he carded splayed fingers through Myles' hair.

"Yance? You all right, mate?" Myles asked nervously. He knew that Yancey and Lakon were generally pretty affectionate. He supposed it had something to do with the whole lupine lifestyle, but he was completely unused to anyone other than Mya touching him. Yancey cupped his cheek and leaned forward to rest his forehead against Myles'. Myles could have pulled back, but didn't really know what to do. "Yancey?" he said again, his voice an uneasy whisper. A warm drop of moisture landed against his temple, alarming him even more.

"I just can't lose another brother, Myles," Yancey croaked hoarsely. In one abrupt motion, he pulled Myles into a rough hug. "Please do this thing, Myles."

Swallowing around the dry lump in his throat, Myles reached around, wrapping both arms around Yancey's back and patting awkwardly. Nobody had ever cared about his wellbeing quite like these people had. He and Yancey had spent a great deal of time together in the weeks since the new contract had been signed. Still, Yancey's deep concern moved him like nothing ever had.

Letting go of the uncomfortable tension he'd been feeling, Myles relaxed against Yancey. "I will, Yance," he managed. "I'm going to join up." His clumsy attempt at levity failed completely when he felt tears prickling at the back of his eyes. He sniffled heavily and mumbled, "And now *I'm* a complete wally, crying like a great girl all over your shirt." Yancey gently loosened his arms from around Myles and eased him back to the mattress, sitting up straight. The pale green glow of Yancey's eyes in the shadowed room unnerved Myles a great deal. After snagging a tissue from the bedside table and blotting his eyes, he finally turned back to look at Yancey, who hadn't moved at all, even to blink. "Yance, quit starin' at me, it's soddin' annoyin'," he snapped. "Are my eyes going to glow in the dark, too, when I'm done?"

Finally, the other man reached over for a tissue and used it on his own face. "Did you just call me something? What's a wally?"

"It's a great sniveling ponce is what it is," Myles grinned.

Yancey chuckled lightly. "So, you want to impugn my self confidence, huh? Can't stand that I'm in touch with my feelings?"

"You're a nancy boy, you are," Myles teased back, sniffing and clearing his throat discreetly. He was quite a bit more comfortable with teasing than with crying, even under the current circumstances.

"Real men embrace their emotions, Myles. I thought you were so much more mature than this," Yancey said haughtily, at the same time lightly squeezing Myles shoulder. "I can see I overestimated your level of sophistication. Well, we have something to strive for then, don't we?"

"How about you strive for getting the invalid a cup of tea, hmm? That's something to strive for," Myles countered.

Heaving a put-upon sigh Yancey stood, shaking his head. "The things I do for family," he said with over affected weariness, turning for the door. "Be right back."

Myles smiled, a warm contentment spreading over him. He'd have to find out more about Yancey's older brother that nobody ever spoke about. He'd have to find a way to forgive Lakon for his sins against Mya, and against Myles' trust. None of this would be easy, not a bit. But maybe it would be all right in the long run, if Mya and Lakon worked things out.

* * * *

North of Blowing Rock, NC and South of Johnson City, TN

Mya awoke slowly, feeling warmer and more comfortable than she had in weeks. She knew why. *Lakon.* She should have been afraid. In all probability, she would still feel fear around Lakon from time to time. Right now, looking into his glowing green eyes, she felt loved.

"Did I wake you, baby?" he murmured.

"No, I just woke up on my own," she answered. She reached up and traced his sculpted jaw with the tip of her index finger. "Lakon?"

"Yes, baby?" he still looked down at her. His head was propped on an elbow with his cheek in his palm.

"I love you," she whispered.

He closed his eyes as if in answer to a prayer.

"Lakon, will you show me it's going to be okay? Will you make love to me?" She closed her eyes, feeling shy. It had been a difficult question to ask, but she felt it was important. She did want Lakon, did feel sexual hunger toward him. After everything that had happened, she felt it was important to act on it right away. If they took care of each other, they'd get through this, she was sure.

"Mya, baby, are you sure?" Lakon seemed nervous.

"I'm sure, Lakon, I want you to make love to me." She took a deep breath. "I know you're not mad at me right now. I know you won't hurt me."

"Mya, even if I do get mad sometime – you know I will, it happens." He looked at her intently. She shrugged and nodded. "I'll never hurt you again and I'll never try to have sex with you when I'm angry. If we don't both want it, we won't do it. Okay?"

"Okay, Lakon." She shimmied out of her panties. He shoved the sweatpants down and off.

Rising to his side, Lakon ran his hand down her cheek, her neck, between her breasts, dragging his fingertips over her rosy, hard nipples. She urged him closer, her mouth hot and moist against his neck. She kissed, nipped, and savored him, slowly at first and then more urgently running her fingers through his hair.

Hungrily, she trailed her hands down his neck and shoulders and over the soft curly hair on his broad chest. She raked eager, anxious fingers through his hair. She welcomed his warm, clever hands as he kneaded her breasts and then rolled her nipples between two fingers.

He lowered his mouth to hers and need surged through her, hot and electric. Her heart beat harder, faster as his tongue met hers. He cupped her bottom and pulled her under him.

Lakon's shaft pushed against her wet, tender opening, pushing, seeking entrance, and then he was inside her. They lay there, looking into each other's eyes for the space of several heartbeats.

She felt him pulsing deep within her and then he slid out of her, slowly, slowly, until just the very head of him rubbed against her aching center. Mya dug her fingers into his hard buttocks, guiding and forcing him to go all the way in again.

Once more he slowly slid out of her. She arched her hips, and thrusting hard, he started to move in deep, rhythmic strokes. She heard herself moaning and heard him groaning in pleasure. Every muffled moan, every little groan that he made added to her satisfaction.

The feel of him as he continued to plunge into her over and over in long, deep strokes drove her higher toward her peak. She could feel him lengthening and hardening, he was as close as she was.

Digging her nails into his back and wrapping her legs around him, she couldn't hold back anymore. She felt her sheath contract around his rigid length as he drove into her once, twice, and again until he froze. She felt the dam burst inside of her and felt his hot seed spurt into her.

Mya clung to him as he rolled to his side and held her close to his heart. She lay snuggled in his arms for a long time before she spoke.

"Lakon," she finally said, "I'm hungry."

She felt his rumbling laughter before they finally made their way out of bed and began foraging for food.

Chapter 15

Five days had passed since the transfusions and various injections had begun and Myles was beginning to feel pretty good. In fact, he was feeling better than he could ever remember feeling. When Mik came to join him for breakfast, he told him so.

"I'm glad you don't feel old and ugly like me, son," Mik laughed.

"As long as you don't *look* old and ugly, I guess you've got it over on everyone, don't you?" Myles laughed.

Ever since the treatments had started, Mik and Myles had been together almost constantly both by necessity and by design. Of course the direct blood transfusions meant the two of them had to be in the same place at the same time. Aside from that, Mik had apparently decided he wanted to get to know Myles better. They'd talked for hours on end. Myles had come to feel closer to Mik Montgomery than he'd ever been to another living soul besides his sister. The old werewolf *felt* like a father to him.

"Here comes Maisie," Mik told him now. "Want me to go?"

"I haven't seen her in a while. No, you can stay."

Myles wasn't terribly interested in Maisie anymore. He felt like he'd been a passing fancy for her and she for him. The truth would come out as soon as he smelled her though. At least, that's what he'd heard.

"Mik, is it true that if someone's your mate, you can tell by how they smell to you?" he asked Mik now.

"Yeah, son, it's true. Why? You think Maisie's your mate?" Mik tilted his head and looked at him curiously.

"I used to think maybe… But I guess if she is, I'll know for sure now, won't I? I wonder if she would have known…Anyway, I can smell and hear things I never could before so I should know, right?" Myles hoped so. It was a big mistake to make, choosing the wrong mate.

There was a knock at the door. "Come in!" Myles called out. It was, of course, Maisie.

Myles made note of her particular smell but he also realized that it wasn't especially appealing to him in any way. Mik arched a brow and Myles gave a slight negative shake of his head.

"Hallo, Maisie," he smiled. He saw that she wouldn't look at either himself or Mik in the eyes.

"Hi, Myles. Hi, Mr. Montgomery." Maisie sounded a little shy. She handed him the morning paper that had been stuck in his door. "How are you Myles? It's fascinating about the gene therapy, isn't it?"

"It's more than fascinating to me, Maisie, its life-altering," Myles grinned. "Only now I've got a much bigger Christmas list."

"Hello, Maisie, how are you? How's your father?" Mik asked.

He continued to chat with Maisie until Myles let out a little yip. He'd opened the paper to the classifieds and was scanning it. Before he could tell Mik what had caught his attention, Maisie hurriedly left.

"What?" Mik asked as soon as she closed the door.

"Mya," he said, scanning the paper.

"Myles!" Mik growled in warning, wanting more information.

"She and Lakon are together. They're going to stay there for a month or so, but she's going to see a doctor about her shoulder next week. They're working things out." He looked over at Mik. The big wolf was grinning and his tail was wagging.

"I just want them to be happy, son. I know they love each other."

"I know it, too, Mik. But he hurt her." Myles couldn't get past that.

"He's sorry, son. He must've convinced her that he meant it," Mik persisted.

"You met her Mik. You know how good she is. How loving!" He growled low in his throat. "She wants to forgive, she always does and she gets hurt. It was for me that she even agreed to sing with him!" he rumbled.

Mik began to speak when the door swung open. "I guess the gene splicing thing is working, huh?" Riker strolled in.

"What're you talking about?" Myles couldn't hear the gravel in his own voice but he saw his long incisors and shaggy hair when Riker flipped up the mirror on his tray table.

He reached up to touch his long canine teeth. He looked at the hair on his hands and his razor sharp, curved nails. "I thought I couldn't transform?" he said in awe.

The hair began to recede and he could feel his teeth changing back to normal.

"Most of us get a little doggy when we get mad. You may not be able to take the shape of a wolf but you obviously have the characteristics," Riker informed him with a proud smile. "Good, another brother to take the heat off of me when the old man gets in his moods." Mik snapped his powerful jaws playfully at Riker in a mock threat. "All right, all right, jeeze," he grumbled.

Myles smiled at the byplay, covering a yawn. He was feeling a lot better, but not great. Besides that, he needed to find a way to make peace with Lakon and Mya resolving their differences. He wanted her to be happy and he knew she loved Lakon. He *would* find a way to get over this himself, but that arse had better beware. In love or not, Myles wouldn't let him hurt his sister a second time.

* * * *

Lakon and Mya sat in the waiting room of Dr. Anita Livingston's practice in Johnston City, Tennessee. Lakon had filled Mya in a little on what had happened when Mik was shot and how this doctor had saved him. He explained about August Livingston and that the renegade werewolf kidnapped Bethany and one of her sons.

While he waited for their turn to be seen, Lakon flipped through a magazine and Mya had spotted a *Raleigh News and Observer*.

"Lakon you won't believe this!" Mya was breathless.

She held the folded newspaper in her hand and was reading the classified section.

"What baby? Is everything okay?" Lakon asked in concern.

Nobody else was waiting and theirs was to be the last appointment of the day. Lakon didn't want to deal with fans or pack members.

"Myles..." Mya trailed off and stared at the wall behind Lakon. With an abrupt shake of her head, she tried again. "Lakon, Myles and your dad..." Lakon took the paper from her and tried to read it.

"Mya, I'm not finding what you're reading about Myles and Dad." Lakon scanned the page.

"Of course not, silly, it's in our special code."

"Just tell me what it says, then," he snapped slightly impatiently, cutting her off.

"If you'd stop grabbing things out of my hands and interrupting me when I'm trying to talk, you'd already know what it says." She took the paper back from him and found the ad again, her entire manner broadcasting irritation.

Lakon winced and attempted to scoot closer to her. She saw that ill conceived move coming and leaned away.

"Oh, here it is!" Her ire was lost in her excitement to share the news. "Myles said they're giving him your dad's genes and blood and he won't have hemophilia anymore! He says he'll be like you..."

"Essentially, they've added Mik's DNA to your brother's DNA, making him a Were who can't transform. You've got another brother, Lakon." The new voice took them both by surprise, answering Mya's implied question as she walked up.

"Dr. Anita! This is my mate, Mya. I guess you've figured that out." Lakon grinned. "This is Dr. Anita Livingston Montgomery, Mya."

"I'm so pleased to meet you Mya," Anita said.

"I've heard a lot about you, Doctor. It's good to meet you. Thanks for looking at my shoulder. I think it has started to heal though."

"Come on back here and let's have a look. I wasn't really sure why you two were here. I'm glad I can help. Lakon have a seat." She led the couple into an examining room.

To Mya, she said, "Go ahead and change into that gown, young lady. We'll just check on your pup while we're at it."

Both Lakon and Mya froze. "Pup?" asked Mya.

Lakon grabbed her by the upper arms and began sniffing at her throat and between her breasts. Suddenly, he sat down hard on the chair by the door.

"Lakon? What..." Mya had her head tilted slightly. She thought she knew what the other two were going on about, but she needed confirmation.

Anita grinned. "This never happens! I almost never get to surprise new parents! This is great!"

"Parents?" Mya turned to look at the doctor and took a step closer to Lakon. "Lakon? We're going to be parents?" her eyes filled with tears. "A baby?" she whispered.

Dazed, Lakon looked up at her. "Twins run in my family," he choked.

"Mine, too!" she grinned.

"Oh, baby! A *baby*!" He began to laugh. Standing, he put his arms around her. "I should have known, but we've been apart and you just smelled so good and – a pup, Mya! A *baby*!"

"Promise me you want this baby, Lakon. Promise!" Mya said fiercely, gripping the front of his shirt in her fists.

"Oh, my god, Mya! A baby! A pup! I want this pup so much. *So much*!" He cupped her face. "I love you, Mya and I'm going to be the best husband and father, I promise."

He dipped his head and his mouth covered hers in a blaze of

passion and joy. Mya lost all track of time until Anita came in chattering. She hadn't even noticed the other woman leaving the room.

"I *had* to call Beauford, I just *had* to! Let's get a look at that shoulder so we can go celebrate the new pack member your mate is carrying." She was all business as she gently disengaged Mya from Lakon's arms.

Mya knew she had tears running down her face. She'd never ever expected to have children. After what had happened with Lakon, she'd thought she'd never have love in her life again.

Even before he'd found her, she'd accepted that she wouldn't be complete without him. His staying there with her and being willing to talk about what had happened between them had helped her tremendously.

She knew it wasn't all better though. She knew without a doubt that she would have real trouble dealing with his temper. They'd talked about it a lot, though they both understood that damage had been done.

A baby! I'm going to be a mommy! I'm going to try to be the best mommy on the planet.

"Lakon, I'm going to take a few c.c.'s of your blood and inject it into Mya. She should be able to tolerate it with the pup and all. That may help the healing process. I have some steroids I could inject but I don't want to risk…"

"No nothing like that! Nothing that could hurt the baby!" Mya was adamant.

"Don't worry, young lady, I'm going to look out for your little pup." Anita approached Lakon and began withdrawing blood. "Your shoulder muscle was damaged, Mya and it's never going to be as good as new. With the injection of Lakon's stronger blood to that area, with his healing factors, hopefully, the pain and the swelling will go away faster."

"How long before the swelling goes down, Doctor?" Lakon asked, slipping an arm around Mya's waist. "Would ice help to make it feel better at all?"

"Why don't you two come and say hello to Beauford. We'll go out to eat and just relax. A little ice always helps swelling and you can make some phone calls. You've both got some brothers to call don't you? And I don't want to be on the wrong side of Elke Montgomery if you don't call her first!"

Mya couldn't help but laugh. She hadn't met Lakon's mother yet, but the woman sounded like a force of nature. Even Bethany had been somewhat in awe of her.

"We'd be happy to join you, Dr. Livingston," she agreed after exchanging a long glance with Lakon.

"Who should we call first, baby?"

Mya smiled smugly at him but didn't say anything. He could call whomever he wanted. She was calling her brother.

* * * *

"Yeah?" Myles answered the phone.

"Is Mik there with you? Do you have a speaker on your phone?" Mya asked him.

"Mya? Is that you, pet? Yeah, Mik's right here, I'll hit the speaker switch! How's tricks luvvie?"

"Dad?" That was Lakon.

"Yes, son?" Mik answered.

"First, welcome to the family, baby brother!" Lakon said to Myles.

"You know I've got to kick your arse, right?" Myles answered. "I have to."

"Yeah, sure, okay, brother. But wait, okay? You've got to wait." Myles could hear him smiling and grinning through the phone. He heard Mya giggle.

"Wait for what?" he growled.

"Wait till after our pup is born!" Lakon crowed.

"I'm going to have a baby, Myles! A *baby*!" She burst into tears.

Myles looked over at Mik. He was surprised to see tears filling the deep yellow eyes of the big wolf. Mik waved a paw at Myles. With a start, he felt a tear splash on his own hand.

"Oh, luv…" he breathed.

"Son," rumbled Mik, "Honey…" He sniffed.

"I'm an uncle!" Myles yelled. "My lovely baby sister is having a wee little baby!"

"Did you call your mother yet, son?" Mik asked.

"No, Dad, we had to call Myles first. We hoped you'd be there but… well, Myles had to be the first to know." Lakon sniffed unashamedly. "I'm going to be a father. I don't deserve it and I'm not sure how it happened, but…"

"If you don't know how it happened, mate, get the hell away from my sister!" Myles laughed.

"You're happy, right My?" Mya asked him. "You've forgiven Lakon?"

"Oh, pet. I'm mad at Lakon for hurting you, of course I am. We'll get past that. I just want you to be happy, sweet. I love you. I love your baby. I guess I can love your lousy, flea bitten, mangy…"

"Hey, boy!" Mik barked. "That same blood is running in your veins, too!"

"All right, I'll take back the mangy part. It's okay, Mya. Lakon and I are fine, right old boy?"

"I'll let him kick my ass, we'll name the pup after him and then…"

"Lakon!" squealed Mya. "Let's call the baby Mykle! That way he's named after everybody! Mik and Myles and Riker!"

"I like it," rumbled Mik. "Elke fits in there too. She'll love that. So you know it's a male pup?"

"Anita told us right away," Lakon agreed. "Our little baby boy is already a month old in there."

"We thought it could be twins but one is just plenty!" Mya said, excitement bubbling in her voice.

"We couldn't be happier for you. I'm so glad, honey. Lakon, son, I'm really glad." Mik congratulated them solemnly.

"I'm so pleased for you Mya. You, too, Lake, really," Myles assured them. He still had a few issues with Lakon, but they would work them out over time. He could be happy for his sister now. "Hey, Riker and Bethany were going to be at Elke's tonight. I'm sure they have speakerphones right old boy?" Mik grunted affirmatively. "I'll see you, when?" he asked. Myles had almost forgotten that part.

"We'll be here for three or so more weeks, maybe four. Anita said the pup could come early so we may not have more than four more months. Take my house, Myles. We'll meet you there. Build on it if you want."

"I think I'll build my own. Not that I don't want to change nappies in the middle of the night, mind you…"

Laughing, Lakon told him, "We'd better go. We're here at Anita's and Beauford's and we want to call Riker, Bet, and Mom – no idea where Tav is."

"Don't forget Yancey!" Mya called out.

"Yancey's right after, I promise."

"Bye Myles! Bye Mik!" Mya called out.

"Bye Dad! Bye, baby brother!" Lakon hung up before Myles had a chance to swear at him.

* * * *

Home of Elke and Mik Montgomery

"Hello?" Bethany answered the phone since Elke was happily playing a board game with the boys.

"Bet?" Did that voice have an English accent?

"Mya?" she whispered. The entire house seemed to screech to a halt. She should have realized that whispering didn't make a difference in a house full of werewolves.

"Yeah!" Mya giggled, "It's me. Speakerphone, speakerphone!" she squealed.

Bethany gasped. "Oh my *god*! Are you?" she shrieked.

"Yes!" Mya sniffled in a muted shout. "Isn't it *amazing*?"

"Everybody! Get in here!"

Bethany hit the speaker button in time for the whole family to hear Lakon growl, "How did she know? Do women have a secret code or something? I swear you didn't say…"

"Lakon? What's going on?" Elke was confused, but then Bethany made eye contact. "Oh, son! Oh, Mya! I'm going to cry!"

"Riker?"

"Lake?"

"Would you like to know what all these women are crying about?" Lakon asked his brother.

"Yes, please" Riker responded gruffly.

"Oh good, I finally get to say it out loud," Lakon huffed sarcastically. He sounded a tad grouchy Bethany thought, but that went away pretty quick. "We're going to have a pup! Mya's pregnant!" Lakon shouted.

Bethany could hear the deep barrel timbre of Beauford Montgomery laughing in the background.

"Damn," Riker sighed.

"Another grandbaby! Lakon's first! Boy or girl?"

"It's a boy, Mom," Lakon told her proudly.

"I'm a month along. He'll be just a little younger than yours, right Bethany?" Mya asked.

"They still can't tell if this little one is a boy or girl but we only have two months left." Bethany confirmed.

"We're going to call him Mykle. He'll be named after Myles, Mik, Elke, and Riker." Bethany could listen to Mya's soft voice all day. She loved her accent.

"I like that," rumbled Riker. "Mykle."

"Are you okay, Mya?" asked Bethany.

"Dr. Anita gave me some of Lakon's blood for my shoulder. She says it won't ever be perfect, but this will help. A baby, Bethany! We're going to be parents!"

"Mya, you have to come and let me look after you, young lady!" Elke scolded. She really didn't sound all that stern, Bethany thought.

"Congratulations," murmured Riker. Bethany looked at him quizzically.

"Thanks," Lakon replied. "We need to call Yancey and let him know. We'll be home in about three weeks or so. We'll see you then!"

"Mya!" Bethany called before they hung up.

"You, too!" Mya called out. They were gone.

Turning to Riker, Bethany studied his face. "What is it, Riker?" she asked. Something was really bothering him.

"I guess I can't really talk about it yet, Bet." He kissed her and walked away.

* * * *

Riker didn't know if he'd ever really be able to talk to Bethany about what was on his mind. He hadn't sorted it all out himself.

He was proud for his brother. More than proud, he was excited and relieved. Lakon deserved happiness. Mya would make him happy. The pup would make him happy.

Riker did know that both he and his brother were even more primal, if that were possible, than full blood werewolves. They had an extra helping of wolf genes, after all. Mik was brilliant, insightful, sensitive, and downright deadly when it was called for.

His father had overturned countless pack challenges. Riker had no doubt that his father could beat him in a pack challenge if he wanted to. The fact was that the Livingston pack and the Montgomery pack separately were big enough for several Alphas. The combined pack was enormous.

Still, Lakon and Riker had been born to the Alpha position. Everyone knew that Lakon was co-Alpha with Riker. But few knew how savage he could be under all that jovial charm.

Riker knew though. That's what was bothering him. Not that his brother was savage – he was pretty badass himself. Lakon was an Alpha the same as Riker. They were twins.

When Riker had put his arms around Mya at the Alltel Pavilion, for one primitive moment, all he knew was that he held a woman who could be his mate. Now he knew that she'd been in heat.

The fact that she'd been in heat must have been what put him over the edge. He could smell his brother's scent on her – almost the same as his own. He'd wanted to imprint his own scent there. He'd run his lips and tongue over Lakon's mark.

He'd challenged his brother and they both knew it. It was his fault that Lakon had hurt Mya.

* * * *

Right Lane, Coliseum Dr, Winston-Salem, NC

Yancey thought he'd wreck the car when his cell phone rang. *That must be why they have laws about talking on the phone in the car these days.*

"Hello?" he answered, hitting his horn when he got cut off in traffic. "Hang on a second!" he told his unknown caller. "Okay, hello?" he said finally.

"Yance, its Lake. Pull over, buddy, I need to tell you something."

He pulled the car to the shoulder of the road right away. "Lake, is it Mya? Is she okay? You heard about Myles, right?"

"I'm fine Yancey. Just fine," Mya chirped. She sounded like she was fine. "And yes, we just spoke to Myles. I'm ever so happy about the gene splicing."

"What's up, you guys? You're back together! I'm so happy about that!"

"Then you're gonna love this one, buddy!" Lakon boomed.

"You're scaring me, Lake. What's going on?" Yancey was uneasy now.

"I'm pregnant, Yancey." Mya said quietly.

"Oh my god! Mya! Lake!" Yancey was shouting and bouncing in his seat.

He almost didn't hear the tapping on his window. The officer motioned for Yancey to roll down the car window.

"Sir!" Officer Montgomery barked, "Is there a problem here?"

"You're a Montgomery, Officer?" Yancey could smell that he was a Were.

"So?" growled the officer.

Yancey's face split in a grin. "Your other Alpha's mate is gonna have a pup! Boy or girl, Lake?"

The officer's face went slack with shock. "Lakon Montgomery?"

"It's a boy, Yancey. His name will be Mykle Montgomery." He could hear the smile in Mya's voice.

"Let your old man tell that to the officer here so I don't get a ticket. Here he is." Yancey knew he was grinning like a fool.

He handed the police officer the phone. He could hear what Lakon was saying anyway.

"Officer Montgomery? Congratulate Mya, my mate, and me. We're going to have a pup. A boy. I hope you won't write my cousin there a ticket."

"No, sir. Congratulations Mr. – Congratulations, Lakon! Congratulations Mya Montgomery. The whole pack will want to celebrate." He handed the phone back to Yancey.

Yancey knew there'd be a howl-out tonight. All the Montgomery's and Livingston's would know by morning. Both Riker and Lakon were having a pup at the same time!

Chapter 16

Auggie and Roland, along with Gil, his sister Cherese and another Were, Billy, all settled in to wait for Lakon and Mya to go to sleep. Their camp in the Cherokee National Forest was less than a mile from Mya's cabin but they didn't want to be seen or smelled.

He wondered if he and Roland had even been missed at the facility yet. The escape had gone like clockwork. Auggie had gone to the bathroom and changed clothes with the imposter Were. That man had shuffled into the library and Auggie had strolled into the visitor's area.

Roland had changed clothes with the other Were. When visiting hours were over, Auggie and Roland calmly left the facility, getting into the car the other two Weres had left for them to use to get away in.

That night, Gil, Cherese, and Billy joined them and they made their way to Lakon's house in Franklin, North Carolina. It was Montgomery territory so Auggie and Roland were more than a little nervous.

Lakon's trail was old but it became easier to follow once they got out of town. Just as Auggie had thought, they were able to follow that arrogant pretty boy's scent almost straight to Lakon's and Mya's den.

They'd gotten hung up at a wide stream, but finally they were able to find the trail again. Now, Auggie and Roland were preparing to sneak down to the cabin and see what they could see.

"It's raining," complained Gil, "They won't get my scent. I don't see why I can't go."

"They already know that Roland and I are out to get them. If they spot any of you, we lose the element of surprise when there are five of us," growled Auggie.

Auggie and Roland transformed and made their way down to the cabin. When they reached it, they transformed again.

Mya had her back to the window and Lakon was pulling off her shirt. "Is it still painful, baby?" they heard Lakon ask her.

"It feels good when you rub it," Auggie heard her mumble.

When Lakon moved away to pick up a tube of cream, Auggie got a look at what must have been a painful muscle injury. *Wait a minute…That looks like a bite. If it is a bite, it's pretty bad.*

"I'm so sorry I hurt you this way, Mya. So sorry, baby." Lakon was rubbing the cream into her shoulder. "Riker feels miserable about his part in it, too. He felt bad even before Dad wiped the floor with us."

Perfect! Lakon Montgomery had abused and injured his human mate. Somehow the other Alpha had abused her, too. And Mik Montgomery is involved! All I have to do is let everyone see it. The Montgomery's will be out for sure.

Auggie signaled to Roland and the two men transformed. Meeting back at the hill, Auggie rubbed his hands together gleefully. He didn't bother to get dressed again.

"Cherese, if you want to be mated to the next Alpha," he sauntered up to her and pinched her nipple through her shirt, "get naked right now!"

"Hey!" growled Gil.

"I stand to take over the pack!" Auggie snarled. "Do you want to be a lower Gamma or do you want to be Roland's Beta?"

Gil dropped his eyes. "Gil?" whimpered Cherese as Auggie transformed into half-were form.

He grabbed Cherese and pulled her into the trees. "Go ahead and struggle, I like a fight!" Auggie rumbled.

Cherese transformed into half-were form too, but she was no match for Auggie. Bestial grunts and snarls could be heard as he pounded into her. With a groan, he found his release.

* * * *

Lakon lifted a nearly boneless Mya and carried her to their bed. Gently, he removed her sweats – her jeans had become too tight for her. Soon, her sweatpants would be too small. She could wear *his* sweatpants. He'd gotten more clothes weeks ago when they'd visited Anita.

"How's my baby doing?" he asked, rubbing her tummy. He could feel the slight curve.

"Which one?" she mumbled sleepily.

He couldn't resist taking a puckered nipple into his mouth. All she wore was a pair of panties – she'd need some of those in a larger size soon, too.

"You're my baby, baby, this is my pup." He moved down to kiss the little bulge below her bellybutton, tugging the panties over her hips and down her legs.

"I think Mykle is sleepy." Mya looked at him through half-lidded eyes.

"Let's rock him to sleep, hmm?"

"Yeah, let's put our baby to sleep." She stretched with a come-hither grin.

Lakon cupped her burgeoning breasts and kneaded them, pinching and rolling her nipples lightly. Scraping his jeans off, he rose above her and nudged her legs apart with his knee.

He slid between her parted thighs and buried himself deep inside of her. The feeling of completion overwhelmed him and his eyes grew moist. *My mate and my pup, right here in my arms.*

They made love slowly and luxuriously. There was no urgency in either his or her climax. Instead it was a loving sharing. Mya and Mykle fell asleep in Lakon's arms. After an hour or so of watching his mate sleep with his baby inside her, Lakon drifted off as well.

* * * *

Tavist Darke was enjoying his visit with Beauford and Anita Montgomery. Although he'd bought some land and settled in North Georgia, he liked to get out and visit his friends. As an artist, he wasn't restricted to any certain place or time frame. He liked the freedom.

He'd been filled in on Lakon's big news and he was thrilled for him. They'd just finished a thick steak apiece when the phone rang. Beauford answered the phone.

"Holy shit!" yelled Beauford. "Damn it! When?" He listened for another minute or two. When he hung up, he turned to Tav.

"What's up?" Tav asked him. He didn't waste words.

"Auggie Livingston's escaped. He's been bitching about Lakon and Mya a lot." Beauford rubbed his face with a large hand. "Hell and damnation!"

"You head to Riker's place. I'll head to Mya's cabin. You said it's just past the small creek? Which way did they go into the trees? Never mind, I can follow Lake's scent."

Beauford would drive like a fiend, Tav knew. Anita would be on the phone to Riker and Elke. He also knew that Mik would be heading home with Mya's brother. Visiting Mik had been his next planned stop.

As he made his way through the woods, he found himself praying and begging to Lakon in his mind. *Please, Lake, please don't leave that girl alone. Stay with her, man.*

* * * *

Mya puttered around the little cabin, almost wishing they never had to leave. After much discussion, they'd decided to leave for Lakon's house in Franklin the next morning. Lakon had gone into town to get a car.

He'd park it at the edge of the woods about a mile from her little cabin. It would be a pleasant walk, if a little chilly.

She was placing candles around. She wanted to have a really romantic evening on their last night alone together. Just her, Lakon, and baby Mykle, nestled safe inside of her.

As she was making the bed, the door opened. Lakon wouldn't have had enough time to get there and get back, she knew. Whipping around, she saw a man she didn't know. He favored Yancey just a tiny bit but had lighter red hair, she noticed distractedly.

"Ahh, Mya Brooks Montgomery. You're even lovelier in person. I'm August Livingston." Her eyes must've widened because he said, "I see you've heard of me?"

Stepping inside the cabin he looked around. "Cozy," he observed. Then his eyes narrowed. "So, sweet little lady, take that shirt off, I want to see what the pretty boy did to you."

"It's practically healed," she choked out.

In a few strides, he was in front of her. Ripping the shirt open he could no doubt see that her wound *was* much improved.

"Doesn't matter, he'll still look bad to..." suddenly the man grabbed her by both arms. "A pup!" he lifted her to his nose, sniffing between her naked breasts. "You are *not* going to ruin my plans!" he roared, shaking her.

"Please, let me go. Don't hurt my baby!" She struggled in his grip.

"Your baby? You mean Lakon Montgomery's pup, don't you?" He leaned down and licked her from her navel to her sternum. "Mmmm. Little Mommy, you taste as lovely as the other mommy did. I guess I have a taste for Montgomery mommies..."

He licked her breast and sucked at her nipple as she struggled and cried out. "No, please no, just leave me alone! Lakon will – Lakon is – He'll be right back!" she screamed, sobbing.

"I wish he was, pretty, sweet, tasty Little Mommy," he snarled. "I'd love for him to watch what I'm going to do to you."

Mya panicked, kicking him hard between the legs. He dropped her with an angry bellow. As soon as she hit the floor, she scrambled backward, throwing heavy candles at him whenever she could grab one.

Auggie began laughing. "You are going to be so much fun, Little Mommy," he leered.

"Auggie, you aren't supposed to hurt her!" Mya knew that voice. It was Cherese.

"Cherese!" she screamed. "Help me! Help my baby!"

"Gil!" Auggie bellowed. "*Get her out of here!*"

"Gil!" screamed Mya.

"Oh, no, lovely lady!" She heard his voice get deeper and more guttural. "No, no," he said in his now thick, bestial voice. "We're going to get to know each other."

"No, please no!" she sobbed. He'd ripped his shirt off and his pants.

She heard the popping and snapping noise of bones and cartilage changing shape. He wasn't transforming into a wolf, her horrified mind realized. He was changing into a wolf-man.

The hand that grabbed her ankle had long razor-sharp claws and was covered at the back with hair. That hair traveled up his elongated arms to his barrel shaped chest.

The hair on his upper chest was thicker as was the hair on his neck and back. In horror, she saw that it thinned and became shorter as she glanced down at his abdomen. His penis was grossly oversized and obscene. His legs appeared to be on backward and arched out behind him.

Some part of her mind noticed that his coat had red in it like his hair and that his face was slightly pointed and so were his ears.

He jerked her toward him kicking and screaming as he reached for the waist on her pants. He pulled them down a little way and then sliced them off of her along with her panties.

"I'm the jackpot winner tonight folks," he rumbled maliciously. "I get the girl, I get rid of the pup and I can still walk away with the pack!"

With all of her strength, Mya propelled her head into Auggie's face. She saw stars as she connected. She knew vaguely that she had hurt him because he roared in pain and threw her across the room.

"Lakon," she mumbled, "Mykle," she whimpered, hitting the table and chairs with a crash.

The pain in her lower back was the last thing she knew before she lost consciousness.

* * * *

Tav had heard Mya screaming, "Cherese! Help me! Help my baby!"

He ran harder and harder. He heard savage scuffling in the woods in front of him and saw a male Were attacking a female. He jumped on the male and tossed him away.

"*No*," screamed the female. "Help Mya! Auggie's hurting her!"

Another male Were came at them and the girl attacked him. He heard Mya sobbing, "No, please no!" and he ripped at a chunk of the male's flesh and ran faster toward her.

He heard Auggie's roar at the same time that he spotted the open cabin door. He burst through it and onto the half-man/half-Were that was bending over Mya's crumpled body.

Tav and Auggie began grappling – Tav was still in wolf form and Auggie still in half-form. Another werewolf came shooting through the door and hit him with a body blow. Tav saw Auggie escape through the open door. The second werewolf followed him.

As he transformed into human form, he heard someone limping toward him. The girl Were who'd tried to help made her painful way to the cabin. Further away, he heard a wolf running and hoped it was Lakon. He called out a howl as he crawled over to Mya.

She was lying in a pool of blood, hemorrhaging vaginally. Tav grabbed something – her pants maybe – and stuffed them between her legs. He wrapped her in a sheet and lifted her.

Carrying Mya, he began walking back the way he'd come, calling out to Lakon. The female Were turned and followed him. She was pretty beat up, too.

Lakon burst through the trees in front of him, transforming as he went. "Mya!" he yelled.

Tav placed Lakon's mate in his arms. For one second, Lakon's anguished eyes locked on his. Then Lakon turned and began jogging through the trees toward the car he'd parked almost a mile away.

He imparted that information to Tav as they jogged. Halfway to the car, Cherese found and had snatched up the clothes Lakon had been wearing when he'd changed to wolf form. She pulled his shirt on and kept the pants for him. When they reached the car, Tav transformed again into wolf form.

"Get her to the hospital and I'll find a phone and call Anita to make sure someone meets you. I'll be there pretty quick."

* * * *

Cherese took the keys from Lakon's pants and opened the passenger door for him. She got in the driver's seat and headed for the hospital. She'd been to Johnson City Tennessee plenty of times. She knew her way around.

When they pulled up at the Emergency Room entrance they were met by a doctor and two orderlies with a gurney. Cherese handed Lakon his pants and he pulled them on.

"I'm sorry, Mr. Montgomery." They stopped him as he tried to follow them into the treatment room. Lakon snarled menacingly. "Sir, it's best."

A lady handed her some scrub pants and she saw a big, red-haired man grab Lakon. "Son, they're goanna do whatever they can. We don't want to get in their way." He led Lakon a little ways away from the group.

"Young lady," the southern-voiced man said to Cherese, "I'm Beauford Montgomery. What's your name?"

"I'm Cherese Livingston," she began. "Lakon, I'm so sorry. This is partly… I didn't know…"

"This is my wife, Dr. Anita Livingston Montgomery. Now I want you to let her treat your wounds. Lake, Tav has already called Mik, Riker, and Yancey." Before Lakon could say anything, Beauford went on. "Myles is with Mik and Riker."

"Dr. Livingston – I – I – I mean Montgomery…" Cherese *had* to clear her conscience.

"You work for me!" Lakon looked hard at Cherese.

"I didn't know he would hurt her. I didn't know!" Cherese was struggling not to cry.

Lakon growled threateningly.

"Lake, that's not gonna help right now. Cherese, just tell us what happened." Beauford's voice and manner were soothing.

"I was mad at Lakon for choosing Mya and not noticing me." She heard her voice crack. "I'm sorry. I'm so sorry."

"Just tell us what happened, Cherese. We've got to stop him." Beauford continued to stay calm. Cherese knew that Lakon was holding on by a thread.

"He – my brother told me that August Livingston was going to be Alpha and that Lakon and Mya had broken up. He said August needed my help and he'd make sure that Lakon noticed me." She felt so rotten.

"He wasn't wrong about that, I noticed you," growled Lakon.

"August and Roland went down to the cabin a few nights ago. When they came back, Auggie was so sure that he had the key to becoming Alpha. He said that Lakon had hurt Mya and that Riker and Mik were covering for him."

"Go on," rumbled Lakon.

"He told me that if I wanted to mate with an Alpha, I had to get naked right away. He told my brother not to help me or he would only be a lower gamma when he took over." She couldn't hold back a sob. "I couldn't fight him. He was in half-form. But he swore that he wouldn't do that to her. He said all he needed was to show her injury to the pack. That's all."

"What happened next, Cherese?" Anita had her arm around her and Cherese was glad for the comfort.

"After Lakon left the cabin today, Auggie got us all together to go there. He swore he just wanted to take her before the pack. Then he realized she was pregnant and that Mya wouldn't speak against Lakon. He said he wished Lakon could see what he was going to do to her."

"And then?" Anita encouraged her.

"He started changing and I tried to stop him. He had Gil and Roland drag me away." She was sobbing but trying to hold it in. "That other Were came and tried to stop him but it was too late. She'd already begun screaming. He said he'd get the girl, get rid of the pup, and walk away with the pack. I don't know what happened but he yelled out and I heard a terrible crash."

She saw that Lakon was white faced under his usually tanned complexion.

Everybody turned when a doctor entered from the treatment room. "Mr. Montgomery – Lakon. I'm Dr. Yves Montgomery. Your mate has a fair chance of survival. We'll have to do surgery. She's lost a lot of blood and she's in and out. She's definitely in shock."

"Our pup?" Lakon whispered. "Mykle?"

"I'm sorry, sir." The doctor shook his head.

Cherese saw Lakon Montgomery clutching his friend Beauford, trying to hold on.

He followed the doctor through the double doors. Cherese was led away to another treatment room.

* * * *

Lakon stood in the parking lot behind the hospital and lifted his head in a gut wrenching, mournful howl. He could smell his father and his brother and – somebody or something Montgomery was with them. When he looked up, he saw Riker, Mik and Myles coming toward him. Tav, Bethany and Yancey were behind them.

He had only seconds to note that Myles' handsome face was twisted in a feral snarl and his teeth had lengthened into lupine fangs. Myles shot across the parking lot and had him by the neck before Lakon realized his intent.

Lakon's own teeth lengthened and he wrapped his hands around Myles throat. Someone was going to die at Lakon's hands tonight. Maybe many. Myles might be the first.

The two men were rolling on the ground wrestling with each other when Mik landed on top of them. His hackles were raised and his ears were up. They had released each other and were on their backs with Mik standing half on one and half on the other of them.

Fangs bared and drooling, Mik snarled, "Do either one of you think you can help Mya this way? I promised that little girl I'd kick my boys asses if she got hurt again. You both smell like my boys. You ready to get your asses kicked? Turns out, I'm in the mood."

Neither man made a sound so Mik moved backward off of them. Riker moved to help Myles up and Tav and Yancey moved to Lakon. Bethany stood back, out of the way. She was crying softly. Mik looked from Lakon to Myles and back again.

"We've lost a pup tonight," his rumbling baritone faltered. "Our little girl is up there hurt and abused, maybe fighting for her life. Are you two rabid dogs going to make her choose between you or are you going to act like brothers?"

Myles turned to Lakon and growled. Lakon snarled back. Mik advanced on them rumbling a menacing growl.

"You hurt her, man," Myles growled.

"I know I did. I'll never forgive myself. Never. But I love her and she loves me. Our pup – our pup…" He couldn't finish.

He felt his eyes begin to fill. Before he knew it, Myles grabbed him and wrapped his arms around him. Lakon could feel the younger man's sobs. He couldn't hold back his own.

After a minute or two, the men managed to pull themselves together. "We've got to stop that bastard," Lakon gritted when he could talk again.

"I'm coming with you this time, Lake," Yancey spoke up.

"Yancey, I think your brother's going to die tonight. Are you sure you want to be there?" Tav asked him gently.

"You guys are my brothers. He's a dangerous animal that needs to be put down. I'm coming with you," Yancey stated firmly.

Lakon wrapped an arm around Yancey's shoulders. Myles did the same.

"Riker, you and Bet will stay here and look after Mya?" Mik turned the group back toward the hospital.

"Yeah, we'll stay." Riker had Bethany tucked protectively under his arm.

"Tav," Lakon said low, "Go walk with Bet, I need a minute with Riker, okay?"

Tav moved forward. Both men knew that Tav would hear what Lakon said to Riker. That was fine. Lakon just didn't want Bethany to hear him.

When Riker dropped back, Lakon slowed Myles down so that the three of them walked together. "You know it's possible that Auggie will try to come here, right?" Lakon said. "He might have some crazy idea of getting both Mya and Bet."

Riker nodded. "I'll get Beauford Montgomery to call the group that helped last time. His Beta got numbers for all the Montgomery's and Livingston's who were there. They have his scent."

* * * *

"Wait, Lake," Riker stopped him. "You guys, give me a minute. Myles, take Bet upstairs." Myles looked at him for a long minute and then did as he asked.

Lakon turned to his brother and looked at him. Riker didn't know how to handle the pain in his brother's eyes.

"It's my fault. I'm sorry, brother. It's my fault." Riker struggled against breaking down. Maybe it was selfish, but he had to talk to Lakon about this now.

"Riker, don't man. It was Auggie, he's an animal," Lakon growled.

"Lake, you're my brother, my twin. I challenged you and you know it. You *know* it," he insisted turning away.

"What do you want from me, Rike? You want me to fight you? What?" He grabbed his brother by the shoulder and jerked him around to face him. "You want me to admit that I wanted Bet? I did, you know I did. I had her in my car next to me. You don't think I wanted to keep on driving? How about when I tackled her on the side of the road? It's a damn good thing she sprayed that shit in my eyes!" Lakon snarled shoving Riker away.

"Lake, if I hadn't challenged you, you wouldn't have..." Riker couldn't finish.

"Wouldn't have what, brother?" Lakon gritted. "Wouldn't have practically raped my own mate – my own wife? Wouldn't have bit through her shoulder? Wouldn't have hurt her and scared her so bad that she ran for the hills?"

"Goddamn it, Lake! We're more wolf than man! You can't do this bullshit to yourself!" Riker exploded.

"Yeah but you can, huh? You're ten minutes older so you can torture yourself half to death with "wouldas" and "shouldas", right?" Lakon snarled. He whirled and began walking away.

Riker stalked to Lakon and grabbed him by the bicep. "Lake..." he began

Lakon turned and cupped his brother's neck. "Take care of my baby," he whispered in a choked voice.

He bent forward and his forehead met Riker's as they clutched each other, struggling with their emotions. "I love you, brother, and I'm sorry," Riker murmured.

"I love you, too, brother. I'm sorry, too," Lakon said to him.

They rested against each other for a minute, gathering strength. "I'll take care of her, man," Riker promised after a minute. "Kill him once for me."

"He's not coming back this time, I promise you that," Lakon growled.

Tav, Lakon, Myles, Mik, and Yancey headed back to the cabin to track Auggie. Before they left, Riker and Beauford had pack members circle the forest so that no one could escape.

Chapter 17

"Riker you have to call Marc, *please* call Marc," Bethany sobbed. They'd been pacing around the waiting room for hours now. Riker couldn't imagine what was going on with Lakon, Myles, and Yancey. Or maybe he could imagine only too well. Most likely, so could Bethany.

"Honey, Mya's lost her pup. I'm sorry baby, it hurts me too. Our pup is going to be okay, Bet." He held his wife and tried to comfort her but it was no use.

"Most of his patients are human women pregnant with Were babies. Please, please, Riker." He couldn't stand to have her begging and pleading this way.

"Hush baby, I'll call him. I'll call him right now. You have to calm down. You can't help Mya like this."

Sniffing, Bethany put her arms around her husband and he gathered her close. "Thank you, Riker. Even if her baby really is lost, maybe Marc can help make sure she can have another one."

Walking outside, Riker dug the one phone number out of his wallet that he made sure he never lost. It galled him a little to be calling the man who would take his place in a minute but Bethany needed him. If Dr. Marc Fonteneax was what or whom she needed, he, Riker, would provide.

He heard the phone ring once and then it was snatched up on the second ring.

"'Lo," mumbled Marc. It was ten o'clock in Tampa.

"Marc, its Riker Montgomery." He heard Marc sit up in bed.

"What's wrong? The pups? Bethany?" Marc kept redeeming himself with Riker every time he opened his mouth. If he'd asked after his wife first, Riker *would* want to kill him.

"Bethany needs you. Can you come? I can't explain it all right now." He knew that was a lot to ask of any man but he also knew Marc would come.

"I'm on my way. Where are you?" Marc could be heard moving around.

"We're at Johnson City Medical Center in Tennessee. I'll have a jet ready for you in Tampa to fly you to Tri Cities Regional here. Someone will meet you. I'll explain everything when you get here."

Both men hung up without saying goodbye. Riker thought they'd probably be friends if they weren't both in love with the same woman. Maybe they *were* best friends? Who knew?

When Marc arrived four hours later, Riker was both relieved and impressed. He was relieved because he knew that only Marc could calm Bethany completely right now. He was impressed because he knew that the flight from Tampa to Johnson City took at least three hours and fifteen minutes.

He'd gone down to the lobby to get a cup of coffee and wait for Marc so he wouldn't wake the women. Bethany was curled in the bed with Mya and nobody dared bother them.

"Hey man, thanks for coming." Riker stuck out his hand and grabbed Marc's.

"You knew I would." Marc shook Riker's hand.

"I did know." Riker nodded.

"What's going on?" Marc unashamedly seized Riker's paper cup of instant coffee and took a big swallow.

Riker put his hand on the other man's shoulder and led him to the machines where he bought them each another cup.

"Hell of a world when even a famous actor can't get a decent cup of coffee in a hospital, huh?" Marc stated then grinned.

Riker laughed, then his expression sobered. "The coffee's better upstairs but I needed to talk to you away from everybody."

Marc took the cup Riker handed him and sat down at a plastic table in the snack area. "Okay, let's hear it."

"Bethany asked me to get you here…Shit this is bad…*and* this coffee really sucks." He took a deep breath. "The Were that was after Bethany – he attacked Lakon's mate and caused her to miscarry."

Riker caught Marc's cup when his hand started to shake. He put his own cup down and moved around the plastic table to Marc. Marc had shot to his feet and was shaking as if he'd been plunged into a vat of ice water.

Riker put a hand on each of Marc's shoulders and touched foreheads with him. Marc gripped Riker's biceps and gulped for air.

"Lake – Lakon – where is he? How is he? Oh my God, Riker. Oh my God."

Riker knew many of his pack were watching them just out of his line of sight. He didn't care.

"You okay to sit down?" Riker asked. Marc nodded shakily.

Seated again, Riker began to explain. "Lakon, Dad, Tav, Yancey, and Myles, Mya's brother – they're out hunting the bastard and his followers. Someone had to stay with the ladies and I volunteered. He could still come back here. Lakon can't help Mya right now. Mom's home with the boys. "

"What can I do to help?" Marc was still very shaken but pulling himself together.

"Take a look at Bethany and tell her that her pup's okay. Then take a look at Mya and make sure she's going to be okay. Bet thinks there's a chance that she didn't lose the pup." Riker sighed.

"But?" Marc could tell that Riker disagreed with his wife.

"She was hemorrhaging when they got her in here. Hell, she was in shock. She's human, Marc, I don't see how she could have…He was in half-Were form when he hurt her. He meant to rape her." The words felt like chalk dust in his mouth. *She could have been my mate. She's my twin brother's other half.*

"Good Lord! What kind of an animal…" Marc couldn't finish.

"I expect he's pretty much a dead animal – he tried to rape my brother's mate and he killed his pup. Lakon usually only pretends to be civilized. Myles isn't even pretending right now. They're going to kill August Livingston. I don't know if Dad will intervene or hold him down…"

* * * *

Cherokee National Forest
The Watauga Ranger District

The four fleeing werewolves paused in their uphill trek to drink and rest a second. Auggie knew that they'd need some kind of a plan. Things had gone straight to hell in a big hurry.

"You should have stopped that Were, you should have controlled Cherese," he growled.

"You said you weren't going to hurt her," Gil countered. "You said you were going to present her and her injury to the pack. She's a human – you might've killed her. Did you rape her, Auggie?"

"Yeah!" snarled Billy, "What did you get us into? Nothing went the way you said it would!"

"Shut up!" growled Auggie. "She was pregnant."

"What do you mean "was", Auggie?" growled Gil, threateningly.

"Enough!" barked Auggie. "The Montgomery's will predictably be out hunting us. If we play our cards right, we can still take over the pack. It's big enough. We can *all* be Alphas if we stick together now."

Roland hadn't said anything. Auggie looked at him in confirmation. He needed someone firmly on his side right now.

"He's right," Roland said stiffly. *Not much of an endorsement, but I'll take what I can get.*

"I know Lakon, Riker, Mik, and my pathetic brother Yancey will be after us. That other Were will be with them, too, I'm sure." August speculated. "We'll need to plan an ambush and we'll need to do it in a place that allows us an escape route."

Auggie looked over at Roland. The other Were wasn't drinking from the little stream they'd found. He wasn't adding to the planning and offered no input. Roland stared at the first quarter moon that hung in the sky and offered nothing.

"You okay, Roland?" Auggie murmured, sidling up to him.

"Fine," Roland replied inscrutably.

"What's up? You're pretty quiet," Auggie persisted.

"Just thinking," came the neutral reply.

"Roland, you know I need to be able to count on you. You sure you're okay?" August was getting nervous now.

Roland turned to look full into Auggie's eyes. "Don't worry, man. I'll be by your side until the bitter end."

Heartened, Auggie gave him a pleased head butt and turned back to the other conspirators.

* * * *

Tav and Mik trotted back to the group outside the cabin north of Blowing Rock. Myles heard them tell Yancey that Auggie and his crew had headed up into the mountains. They had a pretty good idea of Auggie's plans.

Lakon was steadfastly insisting that he be the one to kill Auggie. He wanted to feel the man's last breath as he squeezed it out of him.

"Look, I'd like to kill the brother, Gil, myself. He hurt his own sister while trying to hurt mine – and we trusted him! But we can't look at it that way. They all worked together to hurt Mya and kill baby Mykle."

Myles was trying to get through to Lakon. It wasn't easy. He stared at his sister's mate – his new brother– and took a deep breath. He was a werewolf now, a member of a pack.

Taking another deep breath, he let his anger, his primal hatred of the men who'd hurt his sister and killed his nephew wash over him. These were his brothers, his father – his family. His beautiful sister lay in a hospital bed hurting and bereft, clinging to life.

All five of the men present were killing machines, more animal than man. Their loved ones had been injured, threatened, murdered – they were one with him. Myles stepped into the circle of werewolves.

"They don't expect me. They don't know about me. They'll think I'm human. I'll make good bait," he rumbled.

Lakon stepped up to him. "You're right, baby brother. You and I will step out together. You'll surprise them and with me by your side, they won't think anyone else is as big a threat." Finally, Lakon was ready to fight like a pack of wolves and not a lone wolf.

"You'll go in next, Uncle Mik," Yancey spoke up. "Auggie hates you. *Hates you*," he repeated. "You're a better man than he is and … hell you're part *timber* wolf or something," Yancey chuckled.

"You and I will circle around, Yance. One on each end…Two full bloods, just to piss 'em off," Tav grinned evilly.

Mik looked at each man, long and direct. "Boys, I'm proud of you. My heart is bleeding tonight. I just don't know how we can let these men live. I'd like to say I'm not a killer…"

"Dad…" Myles and Lakon said together. Myles elbowed Lakon and nodded.

"Dad," Lakon said, "You're not a murderer."

"You *are* a killer," Myles finished.

"Dad," Tav spoke now, "This man and his followers preyed on our family."

"Uncle Mik," Yancey's voice cracked, "we can't let them poison or hurt another innocent person, kill another pup. We can't."

Myles watched as Mik, the father who'd taught him more in a few months, loved him more than any other man he'd ever met – he watched as Mik struggled with the weight of what was coming.

"Boys," he said, "I know we have to kill them. I've killed before." He looked at the first quarter moon above. He shook his shaggy head. "Members of our pack. Blood of our own blood preying on the sweet, innocent women who would nurture them – it breaks my heart."

* * * *

Lakon walked beside Myles as the other three went a little ahead of them. He'd been lost in his own thoughts and knew his teeth were long and his hair was shaggy. He stayed beside Myles and stayed in human form.

Looking at the other man now, it was easy to see that Myles' thoughts were no more pleasant than his had been. Myles' hair was styled just like Mya's, artfully mussed and begging a woman to plunge her hands in. He was normally a very handsome young man.

Right now, though, he looked frightening. His teeth were long. Thin, dark hair covered his cheeks and cheekbones. His whiskey colored eyes glowed under bushy eyebrows. He had a feral snarl on his face.

"You know – you're ugly when you're mad, baby brother," Lakon said conversationally.

"Unlike you with *your* dog face," he rumbled back.

"You're goanna have to dial it down some if Auggie and his cronies are supposed to think you're human," Lakon told him.

Myles looked at him blankly for a minute. He reached up and touched his face. When he felt the smooth hair there, he took a deep breath.

"You're looking a little bushy yourself, mate," he told Lakon.

"I guess we're both thinking about the same things, huh?" Lakon asked.

"I guess we are." Myles let out a pent-up sigh. "Listen, Lake, I …"

He didn't get to finish that statement. Yancey and Mik came trotting up to them. Yancey was in wolf form.

"Tav and Mik tracked them up near that summit over there. It's a good place for an ambush. The problem is that it's right on the edge of a cliff there," Yancey explained. "We'll have to draw them down."

"I don't much care if one of them goes over a cliff but I don't want them taking any of you along," Mik growled.

"I'll drink to that," Myles agreed.

"So do we want to go straight in or make 'em wait?" Lakon grinned. He thought he knew what his dad would say. He wasn't wrong.

"Tav's there now tossing pebbles at them from upwind. They'll be jumpy as hell by the time we go up," Mik laughed. "We'll wait for a little while."

Lakon edged Myles away, leaving Mik and Yancey talking quietly. "You okay, Myles?"

Besides realizing that the younger man was violently angry about his sister, he knew that Myles was new to being a werewolf. The young man wouldn't know what he was capable of. Nobody really knew what Myles would be capable of. The gene-splicing had turned him into a Montgomery werewolf. As a man, he was already an Alpha male in his own right; dominant, strong, and capable, though his health had sometimes been a problem. He watched Myles' face closely, paying attention to the emotions flitting across it.

Myles eyebrows dropped in an angry frown and his mouth tightened. His eyes narrowed and his fists clenched. He turned away. Lakon saw him close his eyes and take a deep breath forcing his hands to unclench.

"Fine," he said after a minute.

"I want to go in there snarling and ripping and tear that …" Lakon turned to the nearest tree and rested his forehead against it. "I can't think of the right word," he mumbled.

After a minute, Lakon felt Myles' hand on his shoulder. "I guess we both have some issues to deal with, mate. Meantime, we'll go in there cool and suave – The cocky singer and his jazzy, saxophone playing little brother."

Lakon grinned. "Yeah, attitude *is* half the battle. Between us I guess we're arrogant enough to piss anybody off."

They moved back to Yancey and Mik and slowly began making their way up the mountain. When Tav smelled them beginning to approach, he would circle around to trap Auggie and his party from the northernmost side.

Yancey dropped back, moving west to keep the men surrounded and Mik slowed down waiting for Lakon and Myles to entice the four werewolves into revealing themselves.

Lakon and Myles strolled up between the rocks chatting. "Just a little duct tape and a nice normal envelope, fold it, and Bob's your uncle, you've got a wallet!"

"You know, you can do damn near anything with duct tape!" Lakon shook his head marveling.

"You're an idiot, Myles!" growled Gil shrilly. "One tap and you'll be killed. Why'd you come?"

"Thought I'd like a stroll. The mountains are lovely this evening, hey Lake?" Myles inhaled deeply, apparently enjoying the night air.

"The weather's been great. Not too hot, not too…" Lakon's observations were cut off.

A buff colored wolf shot out of the rocks to their right and landed on Myles' chest. Instead of falling backward, Myles wrapped both arms around it and turned in what looked like an intimate dance step. Instead of crushing Myles' throat, the wolf let out a strangled, gurgling scream and went limp.

"So sorry old man." Myles' voice wasn't quite steady. "I didn't mean to kill him. Just thought I'd keep him from killing me."

"I know, son." Mik joined them. "You really didn't have any choice. You'll definitely need to experiment a little more and find out how strong you are now."

"How'd he do that?" Gil's voice was a high-pitched croak.

"Mik Montgomery!" spat Auggie. "You are one resilient mutt, aren't you? Must be the junkyard dog in you."

"It's true, August. I've passed it on to my sons here, too." Mik nudged Myles. "Myles has gotten my blood and genes. He's a Montgomery now," Mik explained. "Come on down and maybe we won't kill you." They all knew Mik's words would do no good.

"Are you telling me that you've somehow contaminated the family gene pool even more? You've *given* Were blood to a human?" Auggie roared with rage.

"Auggie, go on down there. You're going to die tonight." Lakon didn't recognize that voice. "Die like a leader, man."

"Roland?" Auggie said incredulously. "I thought you said you'd be by my side no matter what?"

"I said to the bitter end, Auggie, and this is it. Either get down there and fight or I'm going to kill you myself. You too Gil."

Roland leaped onto Mik who dropped and rolled, ending on top of the ruddy, cinnamon colored wolf. "Kill me!" snarled Roland.

Gil had recovered from watching Myles kill Billy in what seemed like a casual fashion. He found a well of courage from somewhere and jumped on Lakon. When Lakon heard the other Were move, he transformed and met him in the air.

Roland had clamped his powerful jaws around Mik's forearm and snapped the bone. Mik grabbed him by the throat and flung him at the rock face, stunning him.

* * * *

August thought he could slink away while the other men fought but Yancey had been waiting for him. He knew his older sibling well enough.

"Going somewhere, Auggie?" Yancey said. He worked to make his voice sound mocking and condescending.

"Do you think *you're* going to stop me?" Yancey didn't move. Apparently, upon reflection, Auggie thought a different approach might be more successful. "Yancey, you're my little brother. You're a full blood. I know you're friends with Lakon but blood is thicker than water. I love you, Yance…"

A rumbling growl built in Yancey. "You make me ashamed to be a Livingston. To be a full blood." Yancey was shaking with rage. He knew he had to force himself to calm down. "*Their* blood is thicker than water. Yours is tainted. Yeah, I'm going to stop you."

With that, Yancey launched himself at the light red and buff wolf – his brother, his enemy. Their jaws met in a loud clash as snarls, growls and deep barks rent the air. At one point, August had the upper hand with his jaws around Yancey's throat.

Just when it seemed that August would kill his brother, Yancey raked the sharp nails of his hind leg across Auggie's genitals and down the inside of his thigh. The larger Were threw back his head in a yelp and Yancey closed his own powerful jaws on Auggie's throat.

It looked like Yancey would be the victor but Auggie recovered himself and clamped his jaw over Yancey's ribcage. He could feel at least one rib crack. From out of nowhere, Tav shot forward and grabbed Auggie by the tail, jerking him away from Yancey and breaking his crushing grip.

Yancey saw Lakon surge forward to intercept Auggie. Myles had a beaten and bloody Gil by the scruff and Mik sat next to the unconscious Roland.

Before Yancey could bark a warning, everyone realized that Roland wasn't unconscious at all. Lakon, locked in battle with Auggie, was taken completely by surprise when Roland erupted between them.

Myles surged forward and caught Lakon around the middle as Roland propelled the tangle of wolves toward the edge of the cliff. Yancey watched in horror as Myles only just snatched Lakon from the edge of the rocky outcropping while Roland and Auggie flowed over the side.

Everyone was still, listening to Auggie's plea of "Whyyyy?" until his cry was cut off by a sickening thud.

Now the only sound to be heard in the stunned silence was Gil's helpless retching. Myles still held Lakon around the middle at the edge of the cliff. Mik limped over to Yancey and nuzzled him in support.

Tav was as stunned as everyone else, although he scooted away from Gil and the foul smell of his vomit.

Yancey watched as Myles stepped back and released Lakon. "Thanks, baby brother," Lakon wheezed and began pulling his clothes back on.

"You two go down there and make sure they're dead," Mik instructed Lakon and Myles. "Tav, Yancey and I will need your help getting Gil down the mountain. I don't want him getting any ideas."

"I- I- I p-p-promise, Mr. Montgomery…" Gill stuttered and stopped. Tav glared at him. "I'll j-just carry B-Billy."

"We'll get some of Beauford's pack to meet you and take care of the other two bodies. There will be someone waiting at the edge of the woods to drive you to the hospital," Yancey told them.

"Maybe I should go, and let Myles and Lakon get back to see about Mya?" Tav volunteered.

"No, little brother. You take care of our old man and Yancey there. Myles and I will handle this one," Lakon told him. He walked up to Yancey and gave him a kiss on his furry head. "I love you like a brother, cuz. I'm truly sorry things worked out this way."

The three other men nodded agreement. Yancey felt his eyes fill, but fought back the tears.

"Me too, guys. I hope it's over." He could think of a million things to say but nothing else seemed to fit.

Still in wolf form, he, Mik and Tav headed toward Mya's cabin. Gil transformed, lifting Billy and followed. Lakon, in human form, and Myles turned to follow the mountain down to where the two shattered bodies lay.

Chapter 18

Riker stared at the small figure huddled in the bed. She was even smaller and more fragile-looking than Bethany. She seemed impossibly pale in the darkened room.

As Riker watched her, Mya began to moan, tossing and turning. He feared she'd dislodge an IV or something.

"Lakon! Please! Lakon, help me!" she moaned. "Mykle! My baby!" she cried.

Riker moved to the bed and carefully took her into his arms. "Shhh," he whispered. "Its okay, Mya," he crooned.

"Nooo!" she moaned. "It's not okay! My baby's gone!" she began to sob against him.

Riker wrapped his arms around her and gingerly lifted her onto his lap, rocking her. There was really nothing he could say. When Marc and Bethany walked in, he looked at them, helpless. He couldn't hide his tear-filled eyes.

When Riker tried to move away from her, Mya became hysterical again. With a flash of insight, he realized what was happening.

"She thinks I'm Lakon," he whispered low. He looked at Bethany and then shifted his gaze to Marc. "That's it, isn't it? We're twins – his scent and mine, his build and mine – we're almost identical. She's been drugged – she's going on her instincts and senses isn't she?"

Marc moved over to her and touched her forehead with his open palm. She whimpered and clutched at Riker. He eased her back onto the bed but stayed beside her. Bethany moved around the other side and sat next to Mya, holding her hand.

"Yeah, that's a good assessment, Actor-man," Marc gave him a small smile. "Her subconscious knows she's safe with Montgomery men and you do smell almost exactly like your brother."

"Is she going to let you examine her? I don't want her to hurt herself." He glanced out at the nearly frantic doctor and nurse hovering in the doorway. "She's not out of danger yet."

"I'll stay here whenever you're here. I'll talk to the doctors and be here. She'll come to associate me with you and Bethany. She'll start to trust me."

"Don't worry, Riker," Bethany said softly. He thought he saw understanding in her dark green eyes. "She's part of our family. She needs us. All of us." Bethany reached across Mya's prone form and stroked his cheek.

* * * *

Bethany and Marc were in the cafeteria getting breakfast. Riker had feigned sleep and let them go. He sat next to Mya's bed with his head, shoulder and arm resting on the mattress. She was nestled in the crook of his arm.

"You *did* challenge him, didn't you?" Mya whispered.

Riker turned his head and looked down at her pale face. He smoothed a palm down her soft cheek.

"Yes," he said simply. He'd considered and rejected a thousand excuses in the span of seconds and could think of nothing else to say. "Maybe if I hadn't…Maybe this wouldn't have happened." His eyes filled with tears and he fought them back.

He felt her palm on his cheek. He looked into her bourbon eyes. Mya tipped her head back and gently applied a little pressure to Riker's cheek urging his mouth to hers.

Carefully, tenderly, he placed his lips on hers and kissed her, long and sweet. He explored her satin lips with his, enjoying the soft texture. He moved his lips over hers and tested their fullness. Just as carefully and tenderly, they drew apart.

"I love you, Mya. I love you," Riker whispered. He knew it was true and he knew it was no threat to his relationship with Bethany.

"I do love you, Riker Montgomery," Mya whispered to him. "I'm desperately soul deep in love with Lakon. I always will be. He's my mate."

Riker smiled and kissed her again. "That's just the way it should be, sweetheart. I'll always be here when he can't be though. I'll never hurt you or scare you again. I promise."

She nodded. After a minute he heard her even breathing. He could see that she'd gone back to sleep but now she had a slight smile on her full lips. He placed an affectionate kiss on her forehead and worked his arm out from under her.

He was stretching when he heard Bethany and Marc coming up the hall. He stepped out of the room to greet them. Bethany handed him a cup of coffee and looked at him quizzically.

"I'm going to go look in on Mya," Marc said. He'd been trying to become a fixture for her so she wouldn't be afraid of him.

When Marc slipped into the room, Bethany hooked an arm through Riker's and led him to a large window at the end of the hall.

"You look better," she told him. "You seem better."

"I *am* better." He smiled and gave her a one-armed hug holding his coffee carefully in his other hand.

"I knew that you felt responsible for what happened between Lakon and Mya, Riker. I don't understand it completely but I guess you probably were to some extent. I'm glad you had a chance to talk to her about it." Bethany leaned back against his hard body while they both looked out the window.

"I'm glad, too, Bet." He rested his cheek on her head for a minute. "You know I love you, don't you?"

"I know, Riker. I love you too, so much." She lifted his hand and kissed it. "If I didn't, I would have finished that coffee myself instead of sharing it with you," she teased.

Chapter 19
Ford Amphitheatre
Tampa, FL

"Ladies and gentlemen, we're glad to be back with you. This is our first concert after the break and you know from news reports that our family suffered the loss of our son and Myles' nephew," Lakon said to attentive audience at the end of the concert.

His voice broke and his eyes filled. The concert hall was eerily silent. Myles and Mya joined him on stage. Myles put an arm around his shoulder and Mya put her arm around his waist.

"I want to thank all of you for your prayers and support while our family was going through this terrible time," Mya expressed her gratitude, her voice trembling.

"Our family has put together a melody to remember little Mykle Montgomery. A portion of the proceeds from this concert series and the album this song is on – we'll be giving it to children's charities. I hope you like it," Myles finished. His own voice was less than steady.

Myles stepped back and a small spotlight encircled him while a larger one found Lakon and Mya. They faced each other as Myles began to play his saxophone.

The sensual notes of Myles' instrument joined with the harmony of their voices as they sang to one another and their family. The song was a stirring tribute to the love of their family, as well as a heartfelt lament for the loss of a beloved child.

As the song ended, a significant portion of the audience was sobbing. They threw money and baby toys at the stage. Yancey had crewmembers clean up and assured the crowd that any gifts they gave would benefit their local children's support services.

* * * *

"I told Myles to go on to the penthouse. I told him you'd want to rest a little, baby." Lakon looked at his wife speculatively.

Mya walked up to him and began unbuttoning his shirt. "Did you want a little time alone, Lakon?" she asked him.

"I was worried that you'd be upset, baby. I know it's tough." He leaned down and kissed her chastely.

"Lakon," she sighed. "You're right it *is* tough. I really wanted our baby. It hurts so bad that he died."

Lakon put his arms around her. "I know, I know. I feel that way, too."

"Do you still love me, Lakon?" she asked quietly.

"Mya!" he gasped. "Of course I do! How can you ask that?" *Women! What was he supposed to do? Write it in ten feet letters in the sky?*

"Do you still think I'm …" she hesitated. He was curious, staring at her. "Do you find me attractive still, Lakon?"

"Oh, Mya," he groaned.

"It's okay if you don't, I guess. I wish you'd tell me though so I could try to get used to it. And…"

"And?" He had many responses to make but that "and" had hung him up. "And what?"

"Well, if you don't want me anymore…" she took a deep breath and walked across the room. "I may need a new vibrator… or two."

"Woman!" He growled. "Does this feel like I don't want you?" he thrust his burgeoning erection against her soft abdomen. The image of her using a vibrator had probably increased his size.

"It feels very nice," she said.

"Nice?" he croaked.

"Were you going to share that with me or just play with it alone?" she asked archly.

"*Grrr,*" he rumbled, lifting her and sitting on the couch with her. "I'll share it with you on one condition…"

"What?" she asked breathlessly as he slowly began peeling her clothes off.

He rose up and lowered his pants. His erection jutted prominently from between his legs. Naked, she straddled his thighs.

"I want you to get that new vibrator…or two – and play with it with me," he whispered.

"Really?" she grinned. He could smell how his words turned her on.

He lifted her so that she could feel his erection pressing against her feminine center. He took his cock in his hand and rubbed his bulbous head against her dripping slit.

"Do you want me, baby?" he murmured.

"So much, Lakon. I want you so much," she whispered.

He insinuated his rounded cock head into her sheath and slowly pushed his way inside of her, spreading her wide and going deep.

They both groaned loudly when he was all the way in. Neither moved for several long seconds

"Oh, Lakon, I missed you," she choked out

"Mya, baby, I missed you, too. I just wanted to wait until you were ready. I love you, baby."

"I love you too, Lakon. You move. You do the work," she ordered breathily.

He grabbed her hips and held her while he pumped into her. She rested on her knees with her hands on his shoulders as he thrust. It wasn't long before she couldn't hold back anymore.

He felt her begin to contract around him, cries and mewls escaping her.

"Lakon!" she cried out. "Lakon, Lakon, Lakon!" she chanted as her climax crested.

"*Mine*! *My* baby," he shouted. He thrust twice more and froze, then pumped himself rapidly into her.

She collapsed against his chest. "So you do still think I'm sexy?" she whispered.

"I'll be glad to show you again if that wasn't clear enough," he chuckled.

"Okay," she yawned.

He pulled her down beside him for a brief nap. They'd head to the hotel when she awoke.

* * * *

The penthouse was crowded as Marc's brother, T. Paul Fonteneax looked up to see Elke answer the door. Although there were twelve adults scattered throughout this enormous suite of rooms, it seemed very quiet. Still, it was packed with werewolves. No doubt everyone was listening.

"Myles? Someone's here to see you, son," Elke said. She didn't raise her voice. She didn't need to. "They want to see Mya, too."

"Who is it, Mum?" Myles gave Elke's cheek a smacking kiss making her squeal.

"These people say they're your parents," Elke explain with a twisted grimace, as if she'd tasted something foul. She led the couple to the end of the sitting room.

T. Paul noticed that seven sets of werewolf eyes were trained on the very large man and the hard-looking woman who had entered the room.

"Myles, would you crush this block of marble for me? Tav's going to show us how to make a mosaic." Mya said walking up to him, holding a bowl with a big rock in it.

"That's not marble, pet. It's granite. Old Underdog's just trying to find out if I can crush it." He did. T. Paul could see the effort it took for him not to crush it into powder. "Don't toddle off yet, luv. Look who it is!" he said, sweeping a hand to indicate the newcomers.

Mya gasped. Instantly, Riker and Lakon were at her side. Mik got up and made his way over. Marc, Tav, and T. Paul stood and moved closer to the group.

"Introduce me, baby brother," Lakon drawled, slipping an arm around Mya's waist.

"Why he's no relation…" the woman started. The man hushed her.

"Allow me to present Jane and Eldon Brooks. Mya's and my birth parents!" Myles said with a flourish.

Lakon began to snarl. T. Paul stepped closer to Lakon. It wouldn't do to have him gutting a couple of humans here in the penthouse. Yancey stepped up with a big smile on his face.

"Let me shake your hand, Mr. Brooks!" he said as he began pumping the large man's hand. "Mrs. Brooks, I can't say how excited I am to meet you!" He rested a hand on the shoulder of the man and on the woman. "That contract was a work of art!"

The elder Brooks were smiling hesitantly as Yancey introduced them to everyone in the room, including Mik. The smile vanished completely when Mik spoke.

"I won't shake your hand. I'm recovering from an injury. Did you come to offer condolences about baby Mykle?" he asked. T. Paul hid a smile. He was beginning to get the picture.

"That – that dog talked!" choked Mrs. Brooks.

Mya surged forward. "That is *not* a dog! That's Mik Montgomery, my father–in–law and a better man than any you'll ever meet!"

The large man stepped close to Mya and admonished her in a threatening voice, "You won't talk to your Mum that way, missy!"

Before anyone could move, Myles grabbed the big man by his lapels. "You won't talk to my sister that way, old man," he growled.

"If I thump you one time," the man said in a low voice, "you could bleed to death."

"Not anymore," Myles growled. T. Paul could see his beast emerging.

"Myles?" Riker put an arm over his shoulder. "You want me or Lake to handle this? You know how dangerous you are when you get mad."

T. Paul watched with interest as Myles teeth lengthened and hair began to sprout on his face and hands. As a doctor, the gene splicing and augmentation that had altered the human man's genetic makeup fascinated him.

"Kiss Mummy and Daddy bye, pet," came Myles' guttural response. "You can come with me to chat with Mr. and Mrs. Brooks, if you want Riker."

Riker and Myles walked out with the couple while Yancey filled the group in on the contract Myles and Mya had been bound to by their parents. Every werewolf and every person in the penthouse was outraged when they learned that the twins were expected to give up all the money they had earned for six years, even though they'd been young teens running for their lives.

When the penthouse door opened ten minutes later, Riker and Myles were chuckling. After a little urging Riker explained.

"It seems that Mummy and Daddy Brooks had learned that tax records were public," Riker told them. "They had decided that they were owed roughly one hundred and fifty thousand pounds sterling rounded off."

"Trying to give us a break they were," laughed Myles.

"Turns out they were so broken up about Mykle, they'll be glad to donate that money to an abused children foundation." Riker chuckled with him for a minute. "We'd better keep an eye on the *National Enquirer* though. There could be some wild stories circulating about us pretty soon."

Mya moved near her brother and hugged him. "We've finally come home, Myles."

He hugged her back. "Yes, pet we have."

The End